Llyfrgell Sir POWYS County Library
Llandrindod Wells LD1 5LD

www.powys.gov.uk/libraries

Barcode No. 37218002314297 Class No. ......F..........................

BLOOD,Alan S.
Cry of the Machi

This book must be returned by the last date stamped above.
Rhaid dychwelyd y llyfr hwn erbyn y dyddiad diwethaf a stampiwyd uchod.

A charge will be made for any lost, damaged or overdue books.
Codir tâl os bydd llyfr wedi ei golli neu ei ni weidio neu heb ei ddychwelyd mewn pryd.

D1342691

CRY OF THE MACHI

CRY OF THE MACHI

A Suffolk Murder Mystery

Alan S. Blood

Book Guild Publishing
Sussex, England

First published in Great Britain in 2011 by
The Book Guild Ltd
Pavilion View
19 New Road
Brighton, BN1 1UF

Typesetting in Baskerville by
Nat-Type, Cheshire

Printed in Great Britain by
CPI Antony Rowe

A catalogue record for this book is available from
The British Library.

ISBN 978 1 84624 594 7

To the whole of my family, past, present and future.

Acknowledgements

Thanks to museums and art galleries in Santiago, Chile, where initial research was undertaken, and invaluable ideas for significant aspects of the novel were developed.

Gratitude is also due to innumerable South American and Chilean websites, as well as Wikipedia, which facilitated additional 'back-up' material, especially in relation to the culture of the Mapuche Indians.

Author's note

Although based on fact, interpretations of aspects of the Mapuche culture have been exaggerated in this work of fiction.

Prologue

A stone figurine appeared to hang limply from the buttress of a Suffolk village church tower. Although some of its sharper features had been eroded by centuries of weathering, it had survived there, attached to the stonework, since around 1350, at the height of the first outbreak of the Black Death. The Mephistophelian creature had a melancholy countenance, yet this was combined with the hint of a twisted smile, making the effigy both sinister and extremely disturbing to the eye of the beholder. Nobody seemed to know why it had been put there but there were vague stories, handed down through the generations. One such yarn attributed the hideous monstrosity to one of the few survivors of the plague, a certain non-Christian medieval nobleman named Hugo De Waldegrove. He had been a baronial lord of middle Suffolk and was appalled at the devastation of the Black Death, which obliterated his workforce of serfs and villeins, as well as most of his subservient yeoman farmers, squires and knights. De Waldegrove dabbled in the dark arts. Apparently, he might have commissioned his last surviving stonemason to carve the satanic figurine to be hung at the church to signify the epidemic as the work of the devil, and as a warning to all of the power of evil and the need to pay constant homage to it. Other tales suggested that Hugo and the stonemason were later burned at the stake for heresy and witchcraft. However, no records or graves had ever been discovered to support this. Many thought the whole saga was pure hocus-

1

pocus. Few ever thought that De Waldegrove would ever seek revenge.

* * *

A rarely seen puma was shot dead in Temuco, Chile; while high in the remote sub-Andean forests another mauled and very seriously wounded a Mapuche Indian. The man was cured by the Shaman 'Machi', a kind of female witch doctor, after a British missionary Doctor's medicine had failed. The excitable Chilean news media enjoyed the fantasy conjecture that the mountain cougar was possibly acting in revenge for the death of its distant cousin. There was some confusion as to the exact order of the two events, separated by mountains and forests that, even in the modern age, were steeped in ancient tribal mysticism and legends associated with dark forces.

* * *

A baby boy was found by the vicar, abandoned in the porch of his church, at Widecombe In The Moor. Here, also, a strange and hideous gargoyle appeared on the side of the church wall above the porch. The cleric was most distressed upon the discovery of the infant's body and particularly alarmed at some disturbing markings which were identical to symbols that he had seen in his theological college books that mentioned the black arts. He conducted a secret exorcism before handing the child over to social services who eventually found adoptive parents for him. The mother of the baby was never discovered. A year later, the vicar died a most horrible death. The baby eventually grew into a very disturbed man.

* * *

In a high-class jewellery establishment in London's Hatton Garden, the customer allowed himself a smile which was not a trait that he was noted for. He had previously visited the premises a few weeks before with a photocopy taken from a newspaper cutting showing a detailed picture of a small silver pendant upon a chain. It was an unusual piece and having an exact replica made from such relatively little detail cost a small fortune. However, it was one which the very frugal man, who spent very little of his money on anything else, could afford. He had come to the best in the land and they had made an excellent job of it. The man smiled again as he handed over £520 in used bank notes, thanked the proprietor for his trouble and said that he neither required a receipt nor to have the item wrapped. The jeweller noticed something very odd about the customer. When handing over the money, it was apparent that the middle two fingers of this left hand were joined together.

Later, in his garden shed, the man prepared a crude, lethal, poisonous concoction. He would ask his Lord for a sign to begin the process of elimination with the killing of one of the more prominent members of the side. This would spread as a warning to all of those who dabbled in centuries-old activities bordering the dark arts as *entertainment*, mocking his master. On a wider scale, highly organised crime would take care of the process worldwide.

* * *

Outside an East Anglian village pub, a strangely clad group of men cavorted about in a weird choreography of disjointed movements that bore no resemblance to anything that could be labelled as 'dance' in the modern sense. Their vividly bright attire with, most notably, bells worn upon the legs, accompanied occasional rhythmic, singing incantations and one of them was concealed within the sinister facsimile of an animal. Another sported a top hat and frequently hit the animal – a stoat – with what appeared to be a balloon on the end of a stick. Most of the participants had little idea what their activities symbolised, much less did the crowd who applauded. Their antics, modified over the centuries, had worldwide origins in the mists of time, especially the Middle Ages. One of the 'dancers' understood – and some of his deep knowledge was terrifying. There was an occasion when the stoat keeled over onto the ground and the audience, thinking it was part of the performance, laughed. They did not realise that the person inside was dead and that this was merely the tip of an iceberg of evil.

Chapter 1

FROM THE MEMOIRS OF DR. LIONEL PALFREY, PhD, BA (Hons) LLB

My father originally had the vision of wanting me to become a Doctor, follow in his medical footsteps and eventually enter into partnership with him, ultimately taking over the Practice upon his own retirement. This was sometimes the case, especially with rural GPs, by way of keeping affairs within the family. Yet, following a shattering experience as a missionary doctor in Chile, which demolished much confidence both in the knowledge of his profession and his own ability, he had an entire change of philosophy. This coincided with my own considerable doubt about such ambition, growing up and observing him change to methods which found him at a variance with most of the medical fraternity.

As I developed into a young man I was, nevertheless, determined to make him proud of my academic achievement and succeeded in gaining admission to Cambridge University where I eventually attained First Class Honours in History. I produced an original treatise on ancient primitive cultures, a salient aspect of which was a paper on the Mapuche Indians of Patagonia. I had grown up amongst them as a child in the Chilean forests where my father had practised and failed as a Doctor. The treatise helped my gaining of a PhD that enabled me to adopt the title of 'Doctor', albeit not a medical one, and was in turn instrumental to my being awarded a Professorship. Thus, I proudly held the chair of World Tribal Studies at the small, newly founded but financially struggling Fenland University. Prestige aside, it was not remunerative enough to sustain the opulent lifestyle that my pushy young wife craved for. I had been swept from my feet at a Fenland University party by this young and vivacious blonde actress who was beginning to make a name for herself in television soaps and relished being married to a 'Prof', as she proudly boasted. However, Samantha was never satisfied and always wanted more money, with the result that I resigned the post that I loved and, on the strength of my PhD, was welcomed upon a crash course in Law at the University of Lindsey, which afforded me an LLB degree that led, via 'connections', to a small Suffolk legal firm where I took my Articles to become a Solicitor. It was amazing how many strings could be pulled with academic 'short cuts' arranged if one was a Doctor of Philosophy from Cambridge! In later life, I started my own successful one-man band law firm in Bury St Edmunds. That was after my promiscuous wife had run off with a well-known film director, the latest in a long line of her sordid affairs. Poor bastard.

As I promised my father upon his death bed, I had included the darker side of Mapuche culture in my PhD research and, unbeknown to everybody apart from my closest friend, Dr Gary Samuel, I became a Shaman.

I cannot even begin to describe the significance that this was to have upon later events in my life that were to unravel in connection with mentally deranged and criminal people, some gruesome, macabre deaths and the arrival of a beautiful young American woman. Tragically linked to these occurrences was my somewhat unusual recreational hobby.

Chapter 2

In 1995, the man strolling along a Devonshire country lane on a beautiful, peaceful, sunny afternoon did not have time to respond to the gag of chloroform that was suddenly and viciously clasped around his mouth. A short time later, as he was beginning to gain consciousness, he was aware of his wrists being tied and then, soon, the dull thudding of earth falling around him with the pain of heavy clods of it hitting his chest, arms, legs and face. Finer particles began to penetrate his eyes, nostrils and finally enter his mouth, from which the gag had been removed, so as to mute his gurgling cries in the course of a slow, suffocating, truly horrible death. He was being buried alive and his final, terrifying recollections were of hysterical, gleeful laughter from somewhere above. Had he become conscious again, he would have no doubt been able to detect the smell of marihuana.

*   *   *

On the edge of Dartmoor, two orienteerers came across what appeared to be a freshly created mound that had already started to attract grasses and moss. It was located in the sort of place that more conventional hikers did not visit, but these guys relished dangerous adventures 'off the beaten track'. Here, in particular, they were in the form of the notorious Dartmoor 'quaky bogs' from which there was no escape from almost certain death for any ill-prepared lone traveller who had the misfortune to inadvertently fall into one. Their curiosity was further aroused by the fact that something had attempted to dig open a section of the mound. Earth had been crudely scooped out as if by the claws of some creature. They had heard the reports of the so called 'black beast', presumed to be an escaped, now feral, panther which several people had claimed to have sighted on the moor. Alarm bells rang, however, when one of the lads found a broken silver neck chain, attached to a strange little silver object lying in the hollow that had been dug. Their conclusion was that it could well belong to the occupant of what increasingly appeared to be a makeshift grave or, failing that, to the person who may have been responsible for the strange mound, possibly putting an end to what might have been a heinous crime. Taking out a mobile phone from his small backpack, one of the hikers called the police.

* * *

'It's a body all right.' The Detective Chief Inspector and his team had driven out from Exeter to the remote spot on the edge of Dartmoor. The sky was dark and heavy rain threatened.

A flashlight briefly lit up the immediate foreground, illuminating the blue and white plastic ribbon of the police cordon around the site. DCI Williams was not in the best of humours, having been dragged away from his beloved allotment on a late Saturday afternoon on his first weekend off for a month. 'And a drop of rain would do my vegetables a power of good,' he was in the process of saying to his Sergeant. 'And get that sodding pressman out of the way!' he snarled, as the photo-journalist from the local rag was about to approach to ask him one of the usual stupid questions. 'Tell the bastard it's not often we find human remains in the middle of nowhere on a shitty Saturday and that's all we know ... and no further comments at the moment. Tell him to piss off and take his bloody camera with him.'

Williams ('Willy' to his colleagues) was one of the old school coppers who had learned his trade in the rough back-to-back streets of Cardiff's Tiger Bay. 'Before they cleaned it all up and bloody spoilt it with bloody marinas and bloody boats,' he was wont to say. Willy had seen more bodies than he could count, and now he was staring at a vile, brown, withered arm that was popping out of the soil, and preparing himself to face whatever horrific secrets were about to be revealed as the rest of the grave was unearthed. 'And where are the two bloody hikers who found the dammed thing and dragged us out here?'

Privately, his first thoughts were to wonder why whoever was responsible for this had not just killed their victim and dropped the body into one of the notorious Dartmoor 'quaky bogs'. Nature would have disposed of the evidence far more thoroughly, saving all the effort of digging a grave with the strong possibility that it would ultimately be discovered. Other disturbing thoughts crossed his mind. They were later confirmed by the forensic pathologist who was of the opinion that the body had been buried alive and would have experienced a most terrifying death by suffocation beneath God's swampy soil.

'In other words,' Williams remarked to the Doctor, 'We are faced with tracking down a fucking psychopathic sadist who gets his kicks from the torturous suffering of the poor bastard victim he's killing.'

With a white surgical glove, the DCI picked up the small silver object and chain. 'A memento,' he muttered. 'See this, Doc? It might not belong to the poor bloody victim, could be the calling card that's often so common at the scene of death from a serial killer.'

As Williams walked away to discuss the situation with his Sergeant, the pathologist picked up a small butt of what, at first, he thought was a roll-up cigarette. 'Interesting,' he said to himself. 'DCI!' he called out.

* * *

The old tramp steamer had dropped him off at the small unobtrusive jetty of Puerto Saavedra. The young lawyer from England, with his closest friend, had chosen this more secluded part of the coast as he wanted to make his entry into Chile as surreptitious as possible. They would now face a long bus ride to Temuco and, from the 'Terminal de Buses Rurales', board an even more rickety old charabanc-like vehicle to where no public transport existed. This subsequently necessitated mule travel to the remoter parts of the Region de la Aurucania, in the shadow of the Andes themselves, to the Conguillio area near Melipeuco. These desolate, wild Patagonian heartlands of the Mapuche Indians continued to stretch, even further, over the border into Argentina. The solicitor had returned to his roots amidst frequently dark, high forests, crowned by snow capped volcanoes, and had travelled across the world to find the Machi of his childhood.

Chapter 3

Looking out upon the Green, on a lovely summer's evening, Charlotte supposed the scene could easily have been in Winchester, Massachusetts, instead of a remote niche of East Anglia – specifically, mid-Suffolk. All of the ingredients were there. Bordering the pond was the church with its perpendicular spire and close by were white, weather-boarded little houses. Some were comically leaning over as if wanting to swim in the cool water where the discerning eye would observe some roach and golden carp occasionally rising to the surface. Some small boys with a net were trying to catch fry to put into an old jam jar.

It was very hot.

'But not as hot as New England, at this time of year,' she muttered to herself.

The stunning straw blonde wondered what she was doing here, far from her native America. It had been a long journey in more ways than one. Her husband, a busy New York tycoon, had proved to be a total bastard and despite the luxury of a Manhattan apartment and a holiday retreat in the Hamptons, on the super-rich Long Island, she had left the swine to his whores, his drinking, drugs and perversions. At first, the marriage had been milk and honey. Carl Rossini had come to visit his kid brother, Manilo, who was a fresher at Harvard where she was in her final year and about to graduate. He had swept the dazzling beauty from her feet at an end of semester ball. The wedding had been an opulent affair with New York dignitaries and Senators present. Little did she know of the murkier activities of some of the guests. The honeymoon had seen her whisked off to Paris, Rome and Capri. She had been madly in love with the handsome US-Italian and would never have to work. However, after a few years of basking in sumptuousness and slowly going to seed in champagne-soaked idleness, she began to discover the truth about her husband and to formulate a plan to escape. She still had her looks and a brain aching to be used. Thank God she had her Harvard Degree in English to fall back on. And now Charlotte was going to make full use of it.

At first, she had gone back to stay with her devoted parents on the outskirts of Boston. The suburb of Winchester was a highly respectable, God-fearing little community affectionately referred to as 'the village'. Yet the village she now stood in was the real thing. The church, here, dated back to the eleventh century. It was not a Victorian facsimile and this was the land of Shakespeare and Chaucer and Dickens! Charlotte shuddered with delight. Now she would be able to use her knowledge in the education of youngsters, assuming they did not mind a Yank teaching them the finer points of English Literature. Moreover, the lady would introduce them to some of the better aspects of American writing. How she looked forward to presenting British sixth-formers with the complexities of *Catcher In The Rye!*

Winchester had its limitations and the delights of twee dinner parties with her father's Kiwanis Club pals and Rotarians was simply not enough. The prevalence of religion in the town, where church attendance was almost mandatory, was somewhat stifling for a spirited young woman of intellect. And such was the moralistic nature of the place that the 'Selectmen' of the community voted, annually, in Council, to prohibit the introduction of any kind of drinking establishment or bar. In short, Charlotte had become bored beyond belief until, when surfing the web, she had logged on to an advertisement for a teacher of English with enterprising new ideas at a progressive independent school near Bury St Edmunds, Suffolk, England.

Everything had magically followed suit. She now hoped to forge some exciting new friends and immerse herself in Anglo Saxon culture. At just over six feet tall with a mane of long, flowing, silky hair and a well-groomed, nicely proportioned, slim body, she was provocatively beautiful and would be quite a catch. Who knew what the future might hold for her?

Standing by the pond in delightful reverie, she suddenly became aware of being stared at by a thin, youngish man in a blue boiler suit. He stood some ten yards away, around the next bend in the pond, yet close enough for his distinctive, somewhat sad, face to be recognisable. Her thoughts were interrupted by a voice, at the sound of which the strange youth turned on his heels and disappeared into the bushes that, in places, skirted the water.

'You've come to teach at Woolpit Academy!'

A very countrified gentleman had crept up by Charlotte's side. 'Welcome to Thorpe Amberley,' he continued. 'American?'

Charlotte laughed. 'Is it that obvious?'

'No, but word gets round quickly here. You'll find it a bit different to the States. There's a deep sense of tradition here. We're an old fashioned lot and try to maintain some of the ancient customs. You should come along to The Crooked Cat and meet a few of the rustics. Thursday nights are popular, usually a good crowd in!'

'I presume that's the village pub.'

'Yes, it's the main one. You can just see the gable end of it on the other side of the pond. See it? Just peeping out behind the old weeping willow? There's another hostelry, The Swan And Signet, on the outskirts of the village, but we don't talk about it!'

Charlotte was intrigued, but before she could ask another

question, he bowed, kissed her hand, clicked the heels of his knee-length boots together and started to walk away, but then turned around again.

'I am Lionel Palfrey, a local lawyer. Live in the big house next to the church. Never go there, though, prefer the other alter in The Cat! Hope to see you there next week. Don't forget, Thursday night!'

She stared after him, full of curiosity about her new-found home.

*   *   *

After he had introduced himself to the beautiful Charlotte, Lionel Palfrey stood in the churchyard below the gargoyle. As he did so, he experienced a loud drumming sound in both ears.

He wished he had not screwed up his marriage to Samantha. She had found it difficult to come to terms with the strange beliefs that he found it difficult to share with anybody. She had also resented his almost fanatical involvement with his hobby and had become a 'Morris widow'. It was small wonder that she sought male lovers among her crowd of film, television and theatre luvvies. Now, he reflected bitterly, the dancing was all that he had left in life. It was the problem that had become the solution. He was lonely. At his age, he wondered if he could possibly stand a chance with such a devastatingly attractive young woman as Charlotte who had arrived from the other side of the world, as if by a miracle, to hopefully enrich the life of the community, and he hoped that this might especially apply to him. He had everything to offer her as a wealthy, educated man with his very successful Bury St Edmunds law firm. He owned a large, historic house in a delightful rural English setting and was sure she could find happiness with him. Although he was aware that she would attract the attention of the young bloods of the village, they did not possess what he did and he resolved to pursue the matter when the opportunity arose.

*   *   *

At over 1,250 feet high, the Empire State Building was even more impressive now that it had reverted to its former predominance. Since the tragic disappearance of the previously neighbouring, and much younger, twin towers, it was king of the New York skyline once again. Carl sighed at the horrendous memories of 9/11 yet marvelled at how the city had revived. At night, he watched small birds flutter about outside his window, attracted by the bright floodlights which dramatically revealed the building's famous summit to the whole world.

The air out there was now a lot purer following the severe restrictions imposed upon public smoking. He smiled at the recollection of walking around the outside promenade of the 86th-floor Observatory and smelling the pungent aroma of hundreds of thousands of Marlborough cigarettes wafting up from the cafés, bars and sidewalks way below. Hypocritically, Carl Rossini smirked even more as he took a long drag upon a huge cigar. While his employees in the surrounding offices were prohibited from smoking, Mr Rossini still enjoyed indulging in his inner sanctum. The palatial suite, some two-thirds of the way towards the top of the Empire State Building, was his business home in the sky. It incorporated a spacious apartment, complete with bedroom, bathroom, lounge and kitchen as well as the actual office, a secretarial office and a conference room. Indeed, it was where he spent most of his time when he was not clubbing, womanising, drinking, snorting coke or travelling the globe conducting more deals. This was his world, his power base, and no goddamned Mayor or municipal authority was going to tell him what he could or could not do in his own fucking office. In any case, directly or indirectly, he owned a substantial part of the city and considerable parts of the wider America, with assets throughout the rest of the world.

Carl Rossini was a legitimate businessman yet, as his surname suggested, he was connected to old Italian families of Sicilian origin and, when the occasion arose, he was not beyond using those connections to their fullest advantage.

Rossini picked up the telephone and spoke to his male Private Secretary.

'Georgio, where the fuck is my wife?'

* * *

'Chink' … 'chink' … 'chink' … The unmistakeable sound of clusters of small bells resonated from the Village Hall to the accompaniment of what sounded like a strange syncopation of whistle, pipe and drum music, itself interspersed by some extremely odd singing from gruff male voices. Infused into this was the intermittent clashing of what could be some form of wooden implements. From outside the building, one could only guess at what sort of seemingly ritualistic activity might be occurring within. However, it was all somewhat unrelated to the contemporary world. The singing commenced, again.

> *Oh dear mother what a fool I've been*
> *Six young maidens came a courting me*
> *Five were blind and the other couldn't see …'*

'Chink' … 'chink' … 'chink' … 'clash' … 'clash' … 'clash'. Stamping of feet and, shortly, a rousing cheer which appeared to signal the ending of that part of the proceedings.

Charlotte paused outside the hall and wondered just what the heck was taking place inside. She had stayed late at school, both marking and preparing work, trying to get on top of the job and to make a good impression in the early days of her appointment. Walking on, intrigued, towards the small cottage that she had rented, Charlotte remembered that it was Thursday night. A few weeks had elapsed since she had met the interesting Mr Palfrey and she had been so busy that she had overlooked his kind invitation for her to look into the pub and get to know people. This evening, all of her preparation had been accomplished and it was nearing the end of the week. 'Damn it,' she said to herself, looking at her watch, 'I've time to eat, shower and change and get to the pub well before it closes. Time to meet the locals and maybe they'll be able to tell me just what the weird sounds and music were in the Village Hall.'

The twilight was fading as dusk began to predominate. Charlotte jumped as a bat fluttered close to her head.

As she carried on along the track, the pipe and drum started up again.

Chapter 4

The heavy wood axe fell, yet again, with a heavy thud.

'One more swing should do it,' he said to himself.

Corin Farnsworth looked down at his blistered hands where globules of blood were beginning to form and wondered just what the hell he was doing with his life. Certainly he was fitter and healthier and the fresh country air was generally both sweet and invigorating. It had helped him to give up smoking and the tremendous stress of his former career, that had nearly caused him to have a total breakdown, was finally showing signs of subsiding. There were still nights, however, when the terrible recurring dream caused him to wake up shaking in a pool of sweat.

Corin was a big lad with muscular strength that had been further developed through the work he was doing. He smiled when he reflected that those same youthful biceps had helped him to mould lumps of granite when he had become hooked on sculpting at University. All of his mates had thought he was barking mad going over to the Art Block, with a hangover, on a Saturday morning to continue bashing the hell out of chunks of rock. Of all the genres of three-dimensional art, Sculpture had fascinated him because the ultimate product was the result of a battle between man and stone which was not for little boys and could be somewhat dangerous. On one occasion he had suffered a chip of rock flying into, and becoming embedded in, the cornea of his left eye. It had resulted in an immediate visit to the college sick bay followed by a couple of days in hospital and had left him with a slight but permanent sight defect. The incident had also persuaded him to subsequently wear goggles. He had learned that making one mistake with the stone chisel could create an unwanted fissure that could result in a whole piece of his creation being severed and thus changing the entire course of the final masterpiece. He laughed to himself at the visual image of the phallic monstrosity he had eventually created because of a number of such errors where the stone, itself, had helped to determine an outcome far removed from the original intention. Corin had almost split his sides on a reunion visit to the College, many moons later, where he found his work of art, obviously too heavy to be easily lifted, still lying there encrusted with moss and lichen, lonely, yet resplendently defiant and proud.

Telling the Headmaster to stick his job up his fucking arse was the best thing he had ever done. Nevertheless, today had been a pig of a day. He was soaked to the skin and having to continue working on a tight budget schedule to complete the job on time. With both of the sodden chainsaws seizing up in the extreme wet, the gang had needed to bring out the axes to finish the job by hand. It was back-breaking hard graft to cut the nature trail through the obstinate trees to the proposed picnic site because the bosses of the project wanted to open up the new country park to the public during the summer. The relentless driving rain, falling horizontally with such forceful venom, had penetrated their waterproofs. Yet they were already saturated with their own hot, salty sweat which caused extremely sore and painful welts underneath the armpits, between the testicles and around the crotch.

The lads were totally fed up. Despite the fact that nearly all of them had a dubious track record of petty crime and some of had actually done time, they had shaped up nicely as a crew. This was in no small way due to the experience, skills and patience of Farnsworth who had moulded them from jobless ruffians to quite skilled artisans of forestry and country crafts. He thought the world of them really. They had in many ways, become his surrogate family. Both of Corin's parents had died in a car crash during his childhood and he had been bounced around children's homes until foster parents and a caring social worker spotted his extra high intelligence. He could have easily gone off the rails. Instead, he had been nurtured towards University and Teaching. Marriage became the second tragedy in his life after his lovely young wife died of a brain tumour which sent him lunging into depression and despair that itself, combined with the pressure of his teaching job, caused him to leave and ultimately end up felling bloody trees with a bunch of tearaways whom he loved.

'My balls 'urt, Chief,' complained Nick Bradshaw, the self-appointed leader of the pack. They called him this as a term of endearment.

'Mine are stinking and sweaty too,' replied Corin.

They all laughed.

'Okay, boys,' he continued, 'enough for one day, not quite "poet's day" … that's tomorrow, but enough for a stinking wet Thursday. Buy you all a swift pint on the way home!'

'What's "poet's day", Chief?'

'Told you before, dumbo, Friday, end of the week. "Piss Off Early Today". Poet's Day, get it? This week, we'll just have it a day earlier, but you won't have another free pint tomorrow!'

There was chorus of, 'Oh Chief!' They loved him really.

'Yeah,' thought Corin, 'I did the right thing to quit as Head of Art and Craft. All of that bloody pressure and endless paperwork to keep politicians and civil servants happy. They could stick their GCSEs, National Curriculum and SATS where it hurt! At least this lot appreciate me!'

He smiled and felt happy as he remembered that he was going to the Village Hall that evening. It was practice night for Morris Dancing.

*   *   *

The inter-city train had sped out of Paddington towards the West Country as the young man sank back into his seat and tried to sleep. It was a journey that he had not wanted to make. He was moving from one unhappy location to that of a previously unhappy one. The exercise was almost cathartic and, in between nodding, he was trying to come to terms with its purpose and outcome. The terrain was at first dull, with the last vestiges of the metropolis moving away from the boring suburbs into urban sprawl, before reluctantly giving way to rurality. The trip down from Suffolk had been in reverse, with fields gradually being replaced with the straggle of Greater London. As the train passed on from Salisbury, he began to wake a little and show some interest in the fast-moving countryside, noting the kind of agriculture that took shape from one stretch to another. Leaving the train at Exeter, in the late afternoon, he transferred to a bus that wound its way in seemingly concentric circles through countless villages, taking noisy schoolchildren home. This had not improved his mood. Despite his relative youthful-ness, he was still very tired. Burning the candle at both ends with late-night drinking and starting work at the crack of dawn had been taking its toll. He hated kids because he had loathed so much of his own childhood and was relieved when they started to disembark before the bus had climbed into the hills towards his destination on Dartmoor.

Chapter 5

In 1953, Juana Catrilaf, a pagan of the Mapuche Indian tribe in Chile, was acquitted of the horrific murder of her grandmother who she claimed was a 'Machi' sorceress responsible both for the death of her infant son and her own epilepsy. Using shamanistic remedies, Catrilaf had clubbed the old woman, slashed her forehead and sucked the blood, whereby she claimed, 'A fiery demon has left my body.' Under a Chilean law that recognises justifiable homicide due to 'irresistible psychic forces' she was set free for the human sacrifice. South American Indian mythology is ripe with tales of blood-sucking demons, witchcraft and a history of human sacrifices. The Mapuches were pleased with the result.

About the same time, a young boy whose father was a missionary Doctor lived amongst this society and recollections of it were to affect the rest of his life. Some forty years later, as a successful lawyer in the mid-nineties, he returned to exorcise some of his own demons and pursue them further.

*   *   *

The Tamberley Morris Men seemed to attract dysfunctional characters. The majority participated simply as a pastime which embraced both exercise and socialising, whilst some had a different perspective – that it was the only recreational activity where one could combine copious drinking with demanding physical exertion. As Corin Farnsworth was apt to say, 'It's the only sport where you can drink on the bloody job … one Morris Dance equals six pints!' He loved his beer. However, there were others who joined to escape from something; either a hellish pressurised job or a failing marriage, or to cover up some secret psychosis. These were very sad people.

* * *

Charlotte felt a smidgeon of apprehension as the solid oak door creaked on its hinges. On a quiet lunchtime the sound would have resonated across the bar, possibly in unison with the monotonous clicking of the minutes from the grandfather clock. But tonight the smoke-filled bar was alive with raucous laughter and animated chatter from an exceptionally vibrant gathering. Some quieter, seemingly farming folk propped up the bar itself and looked on scornfully, hardly able to have a peaceful drink. The 'Tamberleys' were in full swing.

'It's always the same, every bloody Thursday night,' protested one that Charlotte overheard as she gingerly reached the bar itself having squirmed through the tight, noisy crowd.

She stood holding out a five pound note thinking it would take an age to be served, but the landlord had spotted the new face and was intrigued to make the acquaintance of the beautiful American teacher he had heard about from his kids.

'Not always like this love,' he said, 'it's just that …' His words were cut short.

'I'll get this.' The voice sounded vaguely familiar. She turned to see the courteous Mr Palfrey.

'Why thank you. I'll have a half a pint of … is it … of best bitter … is that correct?'

'Spot on, my dear! It's what even some of our women have grown to like, under the tutelage of the men, of course!'

'Sounds very chauvinistic!'

'Not at all. Some of our lasses can drink the chaps under the table! Try a drop of our local ale. Queen's Brewery's famous "Black Dog", named after the ghostly hound that is supposed to haunt the lanes around here. If you're unlucky enough to see or hear it then it will surely mean the death of somebody you know, maybe even your …'

'God, seems bloody creepy!' Charlotte exclaimed.

The landlord passed across her beer. 'Take no notice of him. I'm John Harrison, by the way.' He held out his hand. 'You teach my eldest son, he's full of admiration and just loves your accent!'

'Anyway, cheers!' Palfrey continued. 'Told you before we're full of tradition here, also full of scary stories. It's what makes the place so special.'

'And full of bloody anoraks, bloody accountants and such, who are full of bullshit,' commented Edwin Garner, a crotchety old farmer, who was sat just along the bar.

'They call it Morris Dancing,' rejoined another one of his bar crowd. 'Still, I suppose it brings a bit of entertainment when they perform outside.'

Yet Garner was not to be placated. 'Bloody blow-ins, newcomers … all of 'em a ruddy nuisance when they take the pub over like this. None of 'em would know what a real day's work was like, sitting behind desks and playing at being country gents with daft 'obby dancing … bloody load of poofters, they should try getting a fucking tractor out of cow shit at five o'clock in the morning!'

'One of 'em does,' commented the same crony at the bar. 'You're forgetting Simon Carew, the assistant cowman over at Newman's Farm, joined the Tamberleys a few months ago.'

'Yeah,' said Garner, 'don't see much of Newman or his son, these days, 'ope they're sorting the bugger out. Miss old Jake propping up the bar with us.'

*　　*　　*

Kelvin McQuaid had a hacking cough, yet he stubbed out another cigarette. 'Give up old son,' he kept telling himself. Trouble was that Magda, his newly acquired girlfriend, also smoked, and he didn't want to appear wimpish as the relationship was still precariously young. He was also painfully aware that it had been born on a dangerous rebound from his failed marriage and they had already had a couple of turbulent rows. Yet she was the best thing that had happened to him since that bitch of an ex-wife had disappeared out of his life after her prolonged legal battle. Celine had dismantled his finances in an expensive divorce which had cost him the house, the kids and nearly destroyed his business in the final settlement. It was small wonder that he smoked and drank heavily, besides which, it was part of the territory of the successful gumshoe. Yet the ex-NYPD detective, with the previous rank of Captain, was recognised as being one of the best in the Big Apple and the money which rich clients paid him had provided the cow with furs, fabrics and frills to enhance a lifestyle that would not have disgraced a blossoming Hollywood starlet. Ironically, while he kept scrupulous tabs upon the sexual indiscretions of his customers' spouses, he failed to be aware that his own wife, dressed in the most expensive creations from her airline trips to Rodeo Drive, Beverly Hills, was screwing around like crazy while he worked his butt off to pay for them. And she had taken him to the cleaners! 'Fucking lawyers!' McQuaid shouted in anger, for nobody to hear. The sound echoed from within his dingy office in the basement room of a run-down Harlem tenement. He had come down in the world from the luxury of his previous working suite in a tower block near Tudor City, close to the United Nations Building overlooking the East River. He was not far from total ruin, unless things dramatically picked up. Never a religious man, he had ventured to say a prayer in the beautiful St John's Cathedral across the road from his scruffy little bureau.

As he reached for the bottle of cheap Jim Beam and lit another Winston, the telephone rang.

Despite his reduced circumstances, McQuaid's reputation was still good and some of the New York elite did not really give a toss as to the state, or location, of his business accommodation as long as he could produce the goods. The person making this call had used Kelvin many times before, sometimes to track down creditors or, rather more sinisterly, on 'family matters' for which he had been handsomely rewarded both in cash as well as with paid holidays to Miami or Vegas. He was now about to make the gumshoe an offer that would be very difficult to turn down and which might ensure that he would never have to work again. There would, undoubtedly, be some extensive travelling involved.

McQuaid picked up the receiver. Carl Rossini spoke.

'I want you to find my wife and bring her back at all costs. Money will be as much as you need, and more. I have the family honour to consider. Failure is not an option! Do you understand?'

Kelvin looked up at the paint peeling on the ceiling. He thought about the new possibilities of a fresh start with Magda but he wouldn't bet on it. Yet, perhaps the good Lord had heard him after all.

'Sure,' he answered.

* * *

PC Donald Hetherington had pounded the beat all week and his feet were sore. It was good to be back in the village again after tramping the sometimes hooligan-ridden back streets of the socially deprived areas of Ipswich. Here at home he could rest up and be spoiled by his dear old widowed mum. She lavished homemade cakes upon him and further increased his chances of latent obesity with huge full English fried breakfasts, complemented by generous sandwich lunches and monstrous evening portions of his favourite stews and dumplings, liver and bacon, meat pies and puddings. He loved his grub and all of this traditional stuff beat the shit out of the so-called 'healthy diet' of rabbits' food salads served up in Police section houses to keep the nations' Bobbies fit. Unfortunately, he had to live in one, sometimes for a few weeks at a time – depending upon his duties – until he could return home where indulging in the delights of his mother's cooking was offset by the strenuous physical fitness demands of his unusual hobby. The nuisance of his sore feet, however, posed a big problem, especially when it might be necessary to leap into the air. He reflected, with a smile, upon research analysis which apparently revealed that Morris Dancing resulted in as many, if not more, injuries than some of the more recognisable dangerous sports. He took some pleasure in pointing this out to some of his rugby-playing Police colleagues who light-heartedly enjoyed taking the piss out of him. 'Bloody fairies with 'ankies and bells', they would joke when they bought him a pint. He was a big lad and a good copper and they secretly admired his individuality as a something of a character. None of the villains that he clamped the cuffs on had any idea that their captor was capable of executing some of the most elegant spiral, aerial movements in very complex dances.

Donald had been a Morris Dancer since learning the rudiments of it in his Scouting days and subsequently taking it to a higher level after his Scout Troop won the championship at a national jamboree. As Foreman of the Tamberleys, responsible for dance practice, he very much regretted that he could not be there every week. However, he made the buggers sweat twice as hard when he did attend. Hetherington took it very seriously and expected high standards. He also had a nasty, violent streak in him which he tried very hard to control, having once been given a severe warning by his Chief Superintendent. He had beaten up a mouthy yob in the process of arresting some troublesome youths and was threatened with disciplinary action should it ever occur again.

Donald pushed his way through the crowd in The Cat.

'God! Look what the other cat's dragged in!' Corin Farnsworth could never be accused of subtlety.

'Soon be breakfast time,' said one of the other lads, and 'What kept you?' asked another.

'Sorry, guys, got held up back in Ipswich. Serious murder case, tons of paperwork, puts you off arresting anyone. Anyway, my bloody feet are sore, wouldn't have been much use practising tonight.'

He looked about and noticed the extremely attractive young woman talking to Palfrey. She gave him a beautiful smile.

'Nice ain't she?' whispered Farnsworth.

* * *

In a booth in the far corner of the hostelry another person noticed the entrance of Donald Hetherington. The huge woman was dressed in a kaftan of swirling, abstract psychedelic patterns, beneath a mane of thick, cascading jet-black ringlets of curling hair, resembling King Charles II. She looked every bit the middle-aged, sixties throwback Drama teacher that she was.

'Bloody hell, here comes PC bloody plod.' Maggie Driscoll had just rolled a joint and was seriously miffed at having to shove it hastily into her brightly coloured duffel bag. Sitting amongst her gaggle of giggly women, she, too, had been eyeing up the gorgeous Charlotte and was really looking forward to a luxurious drag upon the best marihuana that she could afford.

'Why does a fucking copper want to be one of us?' Driscoll moaned to her cohort, taking a generous slug from her pint of Guinness. 'Good stuff this,' she added. 'Ireland's best, the male pigs can keep their shitty Black Dog!'

Chapter 6

Maggie Driscoll was not the only person who was partial to a 'bit of blow'. A young man, new to the Tamberleys, sat in a deserted lane in the farm's Land Rover en route to the county town. He had only had two hours' sleep, a slice of cold toast and an even colder cup of coffee. His armpits and crutch were sore from incessant sweating inside the loathsome blue boiler suit, especially as he had not had a chance to shower and change his underclothes. Simon Carew was pissed off as he lit a hastily rolled joint and inhaled for a quick fix. It was only cheap grass, grown by an acquaintance in a small greenhouse, discreetly hidden, back in his native Devon. The Suffolk farmer, old man Newman, did not like him and the feeling was mutual. In the relatively short part of the year that he had worked for him, the communication between them had dwindled to monosyllabic grunts in the course of brief requests or his boss's instructions. Yet, he was good at his job and the near defunct farm, prior to Carew's arrival, was beginning to revolve around him.

Although a small cottage came with the job, the money was lousy. However, he could have put up with this if the working environment was happier. The Newmans were an aggressive, rough and ready bunch who ran a very scruffy farm and cared little for the welfare of their bovine livestock. Before he had arrived, with good recommendations from the Agricultural College in Devon, the poor beasts were filthy and permanently covered in their own shit. Simon made it his job to regularly

31

hose them down, clean out their stalls and replenish fresh straw and hay in the barns. 'Bloody waste of money,' the father, Jake, had said while his idle son, Jamie, had resented this new upstart, 'head cowman', coming in and making changes. Thus, his efforts were not appreciated but he only had the animals' well-being at heart. The Newmans were too mean to pay vets' bills unless absolutely necessary and so he had stayed up all the previous night masterminding a difficult calving while his lazy employers slept soundly.

What really upset him was that he had missed 'practice night' with the Tamberley Morris Men which he had hoped would become both his release from the misery at the farm as well as the chance to make some friends in his new environment. He was not much good at the dancing and had to endure a lot of banter from the others. Simon also suffered from the impediment of an intermittent mild stutter which noticeably increased when he was nervous or unsure of himself. It did not help that he was also self-conscious about his social position. The rest of the Morris side were nearly all professional people, unlike him, a semi-skilled farm worker. Like all newcomers, he found it extremely difficult to coordinate the complex dancing combination of 'stepping', 'tracking' and hand movements, with either sticks or handkerchiefs.

'You'll get it in the end,' Lionel Palfrey had encouragingly told him. 'You need to "burn-in" the Morris Double-Step.'

And so Simon had found himself practising on the farmyard concrete, late at night when the others were in bed, and was beginning to make a little, albeit difficult, progress. He became really hacked off that Friday morning after he bumped into Corin Farnsworth in the centre of Bury St Edmunds where he had gone to buy some animal feed which the Newmans had failed to order, as usual.

'Christ you look rough,' said Farnsworth, as he dragged Carew into the Market Tavern for a swift pint. 'This pub's never been the same since they moved the old market out of town.'

'Been up all night, calving … b-b-bloody l-lazy Newmans!' he started to explain. 'I can't s-s-stop long.'

'Yeah, the Newmans,' Corin cut in. 'Get this pint down you, it might help cure your stutter.' Farnsworth laughed and dug him in the ribs. 'You need to leave there, my son, dammed shame you missed last night, there's this cracking piece of American skirt that's come to join us all. Think she's going to dance with the Tambourines.'

'I think I might have already s-s-een her,' stuttered Simon with a smitten look in his eyes.

* * *

The 747 had finally taxied to a halt as McQuaid woke from his disturbed snooze. It had been a strange period of diverse emotions. He had scratched around in Winchester and could have won an Oscar for his acting ability, masquerading as one of Charlotte's old Harvard Tutors to her suspicious parents. Finally, he had convinced her more gullible younger brother that he needed to contact her regarding a monetary award that the University wished him to present to her, belatedly, in respect of an outstanding thesis that she had written. The young man had given Kelvin the contact details he needed and, within hours, as Rossini had said to spare no expense, he had found himself in the lap of luxury in the first-class upper deck of the British Airways jumbo bound for Britain.

Kelvin was tired, jet lagged and a tad irritable. He had never been to England before and was looking forward to it, yet now, his experience of all of the paraphernalia of getting out of the world's busiest airport, with its heightened security procedures, was taking its toll. 'Heathrow's a fucking night-mare,' he moaned to himself as he tried to decide whether to shack up in a London hotel or press on to Suffolk, in haste. All he wanted to do was to get out of the place, sink a few glasses of pure malt and crash out for a few hours. Yet, Carl Rossini was not a man to be crossed. He had demanded a daily progress report and was not even aware that McQuaid had made such progress already or that he had even left the States. Kelvin would have to phone or text him soon with an update, but Rossini would require more of a result.

'Spare no expense,' McQuaid reminded himself.

It was seven o'clock in the morning and he had left New York Kennedy Airport at eight o'clock the previous evening, so that he had accelerated through time during the night.

'I guess this is jet lag,' he told himself. Slightly befuddled, panicky and unsure of his bearings, he now found himself on an early morning Tube train, packed with commuters, heading for the middle of London.

'Fuck this,' he said. 'Spare no expense!'

The train, reeking of perfume, BO, garlic and sweat, slowed to a halt at Shepherd's Bush. Grabbing his suitcase and squeezing, tightly, between heaving breasts, turbans, bowler hats and bandanas, he just managed to propel himself out of the train as the doors began to shut. From the Central Line platform he headed up the escalator and was about to make a London cabbie's day. The black cab sat there in a side street, with the cockney driver almost nodding off.

'Can you take me Bury Saint Edmunds, pal?'

Recovering from the shock, the cabbie said, 'It'll cost yer.'

As the vehicle got underway, McQuaid took out his cell phone and scrolled around to the WAP function. Accessing the internet, he found the most expensive hotel, phoned and made a booking.

'Take me to the Angel Hotel in Bury,' he instructed the still bemused driver, 'and wake me up when we arrive.'

'Gotcha,' replied the cabbie, who answered to the name of Reggie.

*   *   *

In another hotel in a seedy room overlooking the East River, a prostitute pulled up her black stockings and fixed them onto a provocative suspender belt before wriggling into an imitation leather miniskirt and an equally cheap, mock-silk gold blouse. Mistress Mona was back, dressed in the deliberately sleazy uniform of the expensive trade that helped her lure to bed the sort of wealthy men that were turned on by the fantasy of sexual tartiness. In actual fact, the young Latino woman was an extremely rich whore who was employed by one of Manhattan's most exclusive so called 'escort agencies'. Her world was a universe apart from the poor, impoverished, drug dependent sluts who froze to death in the red-light districts plying their sad trade and nightly risking their lives from kerb-crawling perverts. Yet, apart from a vast sum of money there was very little difference between the junkie slags and their clientele and Mona with her multi-millionaire customer who had just paid her a thousand dollars to be tied up and sexually abused before she fucked his brains out.

The man on the bed asked Mona to unlock the handcuffs to enable him to smoke an expensive Havana cigar that she lit for him. Before his smoke, he snorted another line of cocaine.

'And where is your wife, Mr Rossini?' the whore asked him. 'Doesn't give you the kinky pleasure that we do, does she?'

'None of your goddamned business,' replied Carl. Yet, he relented a little, for at least he could confide details to this highly paid bitch that he could not, through loss of face, relate to either friends or family.

'I've got a private dick on the job. Word is that she might have fled to England, but she'll be dragged back here. Charlotte's a vital part of my corporate image, paid for property. Now keep your fucking mouth shut about this!'

35

'Sure, Mr Rossini, complete discretion, in all matters, is part of what you hire us for.'

*   *   *

'So what is this thing you all do? This ... is it ... Morris Dancing?'

Charlotte was asking the question having overheard the comments from the farming fraternity at the bar.

'And I heard a strange chanting, kind of singing, as I was passing the Village Hall, something to do with "maidens coming a courting". Sounded pretty good but very weird!'

She was addressing the question to Lionel Palfrey but some of the others had edged closer to get acquainted with this stunning transatlantic beauty that seemingly the pagan gods from some wonderful heaven had sent into their midst.

'Yeah, sure, it's Morris Dancing,' Corin Farnsworth cut in before the portly Palfrey has a chance to answer. 'It's a silly song that precedes "Lads A Buncham", one of the most famous dances from the Adderbury Tradition.'

'And that lot over there,' interrupted Donald Hetherington, 'think we're a load of poofters.' He nodded in the direction of Garner and his cronies at the bar.

'But clearly you're not!' Charlotte giggled at sight of the muscular gang of admiring young men, clutching their pewter tankards, who began to surround her, as the somewhat upstaged, and older, Lionel Palfrey politely made the introductions. And, not to be outdone, he chipped in, 'There are many Morris traditions and each one contains several dances. Adderbury is one of the oldest and, like the others, is named after the village where it originated. Most of them are in Oxfordshire with a few in other parts of rural England.'

'Confusing isn't it?' came another voice, husky yet feminine, as its owner swept a massive bear-like arm around

Charlotte's slender shoulders. 'I'm Maggie Driscoll, teach drama and all that crap. Let me rescue you from these chauvinistic brutes, you simply must join the Tambourines, *much* more fun than this lot waving their soppy hankies about. We stomp around in clogs and are probably more masculine than they are!'

* * *

The taxi drove into the big car park of Angel Hill, itself dominated by the Angel Hotel.

''Ere we are guv.' Reggie delivered his client with some pride. 'Big one for me this, don't regully go furver than Watford never bin 'ere afore. 'Owever, I likes a bit of 'istory ... this 'otel is where ol' Dickens supposedly wrote some of the *Pickwick Papers,* so they say.'

McQuaid recalled the novel from his miserable enforced childhood reading at Mohawk Junior High in Brooklyn, New York. Yet he smiled a little as the London cabbie was almost a caricature of Mr Pickwick's immortally chirpy valet, Sam Weller.

The cabbie's face erupted in delight as McQuaid thrust £200, in a wad of £20 notes, into his hand. 'Keep the change, you're a good guy. By the way, don't suppose you would know how to get to the village of ... is it ... Thorpe Camberle?'

'No mate, I'm a Londoner, yer need ter ask one of the locals. Try the 'otel Concierge, I fink that's wot they call 'im. Good luck!'

Reggie drove off with a smile. 'Don't yer just love Yanks,' he muttered to himself.

37

Chapter 7

The phone rang before breakfast. It was a Saturday morning and Charlotte was not best pleased at being dragged out of bed at such an early hour. In common with many Americans, she did not function too well until the coffee machine had produced its dark liquid affording that vital injection of caffeine to enable the day to commence. Neither had she partaken in that other life-giving necessity of the early morning shower.

Yesterday had been a pig of a day, beginning with a hangover from too much of that goddammed 'old socks' or whatever they called their beloved strong ale. She had gone to school with a slight headache that had blossomed into a stinker by the afternoon, at which time she discovered just how cruelly unforgiving British adolescents could be, even if they were from well-bred homes. The little bastards had failed to appreciate the finer points of *Romeo And Juliet* and, frankly, she could have pushed Juliet off that bloody balcony feeling the way she did. The solution was a lovely hot bath, a cup of chocolate and a good night's sleep. Everything went to plan until she was disturbed at what seemed the crack of dawn by some idiot on the phone. In actual fact it had just turned nine o'clock in the morning.

'Yah!' Charlotte snapped into the mouthpiece.

''Ello luv,' said a smoky, husky voice. 'Hope I haven't got you up! Didn't have much time to talk to you on Thursday night, got your number from old Palfrey and just wanted to get to know you better ... and try to persuade you to join the ladies' "cloggies". You'd have a load of fun and would certainly find out about eccentric British tradition. Besides, we can give those men a run for their money! I'll drop by and pick you up, take you for lunch, say around 12.30? That's if you've nothing else planned?'

It was the unmistakeable, commandingly persuasive voice of Maggie Driscoll. Almost a *fait accompli*!

'Er, no that'll be fine, looking forward to it!' Charlotte replied, feeling almost guilty about her aggressive manner when she had answered the call; or was it that some people just seemed to have that edge of control over others?

She quickly jumped into an old baggy T-shirt, jeans and a pair of flip-flops, filled and switched on the coffee machine for later, before heading out of the cottage for a breath of fresh air.

* * *

Simon Carew was excited. His life had been relatively shallow. Brought up by adoptive parents in the wilderness of Dartmoor, he was a somewhat lonely, morose child who lived in the shadow of their real son, his elder half-brother, whom he hated. Despite his parents trying to give him all the love they could, he seemed to reject affection, preferring the isolation of the moor and the wildlife that inhabited it. They were relieved when he finally quit the family smallholding to go to Agricultural College to train to be a stockman. From there he left with a basic farm worker's qualification in animal husbandry and moved on to his first job with the miserable Newmans.

Carew had never had a proper relationship with a girl and his attempts at trying to woo the opposite sex were generally unsuccessful. One serious date that he had with a fat cleaning lady at the college ended with some fumbled groping in the back row of a cinema. This earned him a slap in the face and a long walk home as her car had been the means of transport.

The prospect of meeting an American girl filled him with anticipation. In his naïve way he thought that maybe she would be different to British lasses and that he might just be able to impress her with his Devon accent and knowledge of animals.

'All women love animals, don't they?' he reasoned to himself.

* * *

Kelvin McQuaid awoke with a mouth like an orang-utan's rectum and a headache which resembled an explosion in a matchstick factory.

It had been a good night. He had struck up an affinity with the hotel Concierge, who had a liking for Americans, or maybe he was anticipating a substantial tip at the end of his stay. He had already informed McQuaid that there was only one bus a week to Thorpe Amberley and that the only taxis were invariably fully booked and usually needed a few days' notice for any journeys beyond Bury, out into the countryside. Nevertheless, Arnold ('Call me Arnie,' the man had said) insisted that as McQuaid would have to wait around for a couple of days, he needed a bit of old-fashioned Suffolk hospitality. 'And you need a good piss-up after all that travel-ling,' the Concierge had declared, adding that he was off duty at eight that evening and that he would take McQuaid around the town. 'We've the best pubs and beer in the whole of England.' Thus, after a couple of hours' kip and a huge meal of traditional steak and kidney pie, with lashings of veg and gravy, McQuaid was fit for the challenge. However, after years of consuming pasteurised, canned Yankee beers he was not prepared for the onslaught of strong real ale straight from a wooden barrel. 'Gee, this is great!' he had enthused at the time.

Now he was suffering and had to face the horrors of what

they described as a 'full English'. As he stared forlornly at the massive plate of sausages, bacon, eggs, beans and fried bread, that seemed to be swimming in grease, his heart sank. He wistfully thought about the fruit bowl of sliced red melon, apples, tangerines, and so on, complemented by a small pot of cottage cheese and followed by the much healthier lightly boiled over-easy eggs and tomatoes, with delicately prepared pancakes, that he was accustomed to back home. 'Why the fuck am I in this godforsaken country?' he asked himself. He wished later that, had he not felt so rough, he might have requested something that resembled an American breakfast which the hotel would surely have accommodated.

His thoughts were interrupted by the ever-exuberant Arnie. 'How are we squire?' enquired the Concierge behind him. 'Think I've solved your transportation problem. There's a mate of mine who can run you out to Thorpey tomorrow, nothing fancy, it's an old truck, but it'll get you there. He only wants a tenner!'

Kelvin nodded and smiled, politely, while chewing some gristly, fatty bacon and feeling quite sick.

'That'll do you good, mate,' laughed Arnie. 'We'll have a hair of the dog in the bar at lunchtime.'

'Bloody mad Brits,' McQuaid muttered under his breath. 'Yeah, sure,' he replied, slightly grimacing at the thought.

*   *   *

After the rude awakening of Maggie's early morning call, Charlotte had decided that a brisk walk was urgently needed to clear her head and put thoughts into perspective. She had taken a quick tour around the village. This would also give her a slight appetite for a hurried breakfast of toast and marmalade with gallons of strong coffee before attempting to get ready for an assignation that she was not particularly looking forward to yet, concerning which, she was curiously intrigued.

After skirting around the pond and passing Lionel Palfrey's house, she came upon the church which she had never really had a chance to explore, although now was certainly not the time to do it. Nevertheless, looking up at the tower, she was a aware of a sinister figurine strangely attached, in an unexpected position, to one of the support buttresses. It was more than just a gargoyle and, even more fascinating was that its quite large face reminded Charlotte of somebody she had encountered in the area. She shuddered a little as, most frustratingly, she could not recall who the face belonged to. There had to be some explanation. Maybe Ms Driscoll would have some knowledge of it.

Charlotte did not know why she had hurriedly dolled herself up. She was not going to be swept off her feet by some gorgeous hunk or, maybe, even Corin Farnsworth, who she found quite attractive. Instead, she was to be obviously wooed by a plump lump who she suspected might have a preference for her own sex to that of men. In which case Maggie would be sadly disappointed because Charlotte was dead straight. Nevertheless, feminine pride had transformed her into looking the million dollars that would no doubt have Ms Driscoll drooling into her Guinness. Her chic leather bomber jacket covered a seductive little silk top, revealing some bare midriff and complemented by a pair of skin-tight leather trousers tucked into knee-length stiletto-heeled boots.

As the Drama teacher's old Mark I Spitfire roared into Charlotte's driveway, a pair of eyes peered from behind some bushes.

'You l-l-ook f-f-fucking b-b-beautiful,' stuttered the voice below the eyes.

* * *

43

The early afternoon market day bus from Bury St Edmunds to the surrounding villages had to be seen to be believed. It was a cacophony of noise and rustic fuss. Passengers stumbled over antediluvian carpet bags stuffed with worthless collectables purchased at the morning's bric-a-brac auctions. Two small goats were each tied by a short length of rope to one of the back seats. Chickens and ducks squawked and quacked in some strange harmony from the hessian sacks in which they were temporarily imprisoned.

''Ang on fer me droiver!' yelled a fat old farmer's wife as she clambered aboard to the clanging tune of the pots and pans tied around her neck with string. 'Bargain these!' she announced to everyone as she squeezed her enormous frame into the only available seat.

This was a far cry from that other mayhem of Manhattan. McQuaid had to metaphorically pinch himself to confirm that it was real. Part of him wanted to murder that twat Arnie, the stupid Concierge. 'Sorry mate,' he had apologised that morning, 'my mate can't take yer today, he got nicked by the law fer 'aving bald tyres. Never mind, though, it's market day and you can take the return bus.'

Yet another part of him wanted to thank the daft bastard because he would not have missed this impromptu entertainment for the world. He had checked out of the 'Angel' and hoped that he would find accommodation of sorts in, or around, Thorpe Amberley.

Once the bus had passed Bury's distinctive little Cathedral, the Abbey ruins and the huge Norman Tower, rumbling away from the tangle of medieval streets, the hubbub started to quieten down. As the vehicle moved out into the rolling open countryside to the east of the town, Kelvin plucked up the courage to address the farmer's wife who had plonked her massive backside onto the seat next to his on the opposite side of the cluttered central aisle.

''Scuse me honey,' he piped up in a strong Brooklyn

voice, 'is this the correct bus for Thorpe Camberwell?'

'Cooey, a Yankee accent,' the women shrilled, loudly, to be heard by every passenger.

'You mean Thorpe Amberley,' said another gruff voice.

'Yeah, well I keep getting your British names muddled up.'

The elderly gentleman spoke again. He was quite sophisticated. 'There's another American there, a woman, quite a coincidence. We don't get many foreigners in these parts.'

The bus had stopped at both Woolpit and Walsham-le-Willows to alight most of the passengers, their livestock, knick-knacks and jumble.

'Now it's past Wolshum, it'll press on, eventually, to Thorpe Amberley,' added the robust farmer's wife as the dilapidated vehicle seemed to lose itself in a labyrinth of winding country lanes that had no fixed direction.

'Bit off the beaten track, luv,' she added.

McQuaid's heart skipped a beat. Now he knew he was on the *right* track.

* * *

'God, you look stunning!'

Maggie Driscoll gazed upon the beautiful vision of the divine creature who answered the door and immediately felt a surge of horniness flow through her own decadent body. Although she had made an effort to depart from her usual flouncy, arty, gear, the leader of the Tambourines wondered if Charlotte would ever fancy her, let alone share a bed.

'Look different yourself,' responded Charlotte at the sight of the woman clad in a charity shop beige trouser suit that was normally reserved for school parents' evenings. Driscoll had made an effort to impress.

It was a breezy drive in the open-top Spitfire to a pleasant little hostelry by the side of a small river that, itself, was a tributary of the Waveney that eventually flowed into the sea at Lowestoft.

'Nice spot,' commented Charlotte as they began to settle into an al fresco ploughman's, watching the swans drift by in the midday sunshine. 'So we're both teachers then?'

'Yeah, but you're in the more cushy sector; private education, eh? I teach the peasantry at a big 'comp' in Ipswich. Little big bastards mostly, God bless 'em, none of your twelve kids to a class stuff that I expect you're used to!'

'Well ... . it's not all that good,' protested the American. 'I had a rough day yesterday, *Romeo And Juliet*, hung over!'

They both laughed.

'Enough of this shop talk,' said Maggie. 'Tell me about yourself.'

'Before I begin,' Charlotte replied, 'I've one or two questions to ask you.'

* * *

In New York, Carl Rossini was just about to be given a blow job by another of his highly paid whores, when the phone rang.

'Sort the bitch out!' he barked down the mouthpiece.

McQuaid waited before replying.

'Now that I've found out where your wife is, it's got to be done properly, otherwise the whole thing could badly misfire. I've got to work around her, gain her confidence and masquerade as somebody else. Trust me!'

* * *

The church clock tower struck three o'clock. It was that early hour of the Suffolk morning which fitted between the two main time zones of Thorpe Amberley's human activity. The late night illicit 'OT' drinkers of Edwin Garner's bar-propping buddies at The Cat had long since departed towards their alcoholic slumber. And the extremely early morning work schedules of the farming milking routine, the milkman's round and the sorting of the newspapers and post in the village stores cum post office had not yet begun. In all probability, the village was still blissfully asleep, apart from one solitary soul.

As the moon briefly appeared from behind a troublesome dark bank of cumulonimbus which threatened a later morning downpour, its bright, translucent, pale blue light illuminated the figurine on the church tower buttress. The kneeling body, below, implored to the effigy as it nodded assent.

'Give me another sign, Master! I know what I must do ... his name is Farnsworth ... just the right choice ... a popular leading member ...'

Chapter 8

Every Morris side has a number of characters with a distinct role to play, as distinguished from the rest of the dancers. In the Tamberleys, the leader of the troupe, in common with all Morris sides, was the 'Squire', in the person of Lionel Palfrey, who made all the major decisions such as venues for performing and liaison with the public and media in general. The 'Foreman', Donald Hetherington, a dancer since boyhood, was responsible for all the rigorous weekly practising, even if Police duties prevented him from being there some weeks. In his absence, Palfrey himself would take over, although Donald thought he was too soft and a little 'past it'. 'We don't want to look like a bunch of big girls' blouses in front of our audiences,' was the policeman's favourite expression when giving someone a bollocking. 'No wonder he's a bloody copper,' some would mutter under their breath, or, 'Probably trained in the fucking Gestapo,' was a typical comment.

Financial matters were dealt with by the 'Bagman', a diminutive skinny little fellow, Reginald Walden, who was an accountant and, thus, well suited to the job. He was competent at coaxing people into coughing up their 'subs' or engaging in extra fundraising activities, sometimes with a veiled threat. Yet Walden was a loner and very rarely joined the rest for drinks in the pub after practice or dancing out. He was a dark character and a serious oddball.

Corin Farnsworth was the 'Fool', which required him to be as nimble on his feet as he was heavy-handed with the wood axe. The role demanded both extensive dancing experience combined with some comic acting-cum-clowning ability and lots of imagination. He was frequently the much-loved star of the show, especially by the kids, for belting everybody with his homemade 'pig's bladder' on a stick. The target for this was often the 'Animal', another popular character with all Morris sides. The creature adopted by the Tamberley Morris Men was a stoat, moulded from strong papier-mâché and reinforced and laminated by layers of gloss paint. The animalistic design was painted on top of that. To go inside was an onerous task shared, in rotation, by each of the other dancers. Bearing the cumbersome creature upon one's body, as well as attempting the dancing, was a sure-fire way to lose some weight. 'Half a bloody stone I lost the last time I was that thing,' complained Hetherington, who had had to stand in for one of the dancers who was once taken ill before a dance out. Occasionally, the Fool and the Animal would perform a 'double act' with the Fool chasing the Stoat around the dance arena. Inside the Stoat was a string pulley that activated a lever to open and shut the creature's mouth so that spectators, children in particular, could put coins in to bolster the Tamberley funds. The money would slide down a chute into a container fixed to the inside of the body and the kids loved to laugh at the sound of it hitting the bottom.

The Tamberleys also featured a more exclusive musical sound in the playing of diverse, ancient tunes. Whereas the majority of Morris sides used accordion or concertina 'squeezebox' accompaniment, and sometimes a fiddle, the men from Thorpe Amberley employed the simple 'tabor and whistle' which had a much more medieval effect, reminiscent of mummers and mystery plays. The musician was a non-dancing Bury St Edmunds cathedral organist, John Hopper, who forsook his religious calling to play 'pagan rubbish', as it was described by his scornful Bishop who strongly disapproved but could not dismiss one of the best church musicians in Suffolk.

Chapter 9

FROM THE MEMOIRS OF DR. LIONEL PALFREY, PhD, BA (Hons) LLB

I had travelled inland through forested valleys, from which popped up smaller mountains that appeared blue, shrouded in misty clouds, below the higher snow-capped volcanoes and the Andes themselves. Here, in these menacing, remote communities, resurrecting disturbing childhood memories, I now fully learned the basis of ritualistic killings and cures, some of which were too horrific to think about, such as one coastal-dwelling Machi who ordered the severing of arms and legs and sticking the mutilated torso into the sand to be washed away by the waters of the Pacific.

*'Meezta Lionel,' a shrivelled, wizened life form, squatting in the doorway of her **Ruka**, had rasped at me.*

The Machi barely spoke English but the old lady's remarkable powers recalled, from seeing me, the man before her, the face of the small boy who, thirty years ago, had sat upon his father's knee: he, who as a Doctor, had failed to cure one of the tribe yet witnessed an amazing resurrection of life from certain death.

The rest of our conversation was conducted through my interpreter and companion, Dr Gary Samuel, who had gained his PhD partly through the study of the languages of indigenous peoples in the Americas. We had met at Cambridge and had remained firm friends ever since. Gary also shared my passionate interest in occult ritualism.

'You want, I teach you kill,' she had said.

'And to cure,' I had replied excitedly.

I conveyed to the Machi that my principal interest was in curative shamanism but that I would not be averse to receiving knowledge of methods of killing which might be useful in what I saw as a world of ever-burgeoning violence.

Before leaving Chile, I possessed sufficient, quite terrifying, knowledge to enable me to secretly indulge in dabbling with the **wekufe** *evil spirits dominating the* **kalku***, or the devilish side of the Mapuche Indians' shamanistic beliefs. Yet this frequently involved the sacrifice of a rare animal and, as a member of the RSPCA, it bothered me greatly. More significantly, I knew how to terrify adversaries before committing them to a violent death. Dr. Lionel Palfrey, PhD, BA (Hons), LLB, now knew how to kill.*

I also observed traditional Chilean dancing, partly associated with the Mapuches and concluded that the waving of handkerchiefs, together with many of the stepping and tracking patterns of the dances, bore strong resemblance to the Morris and its pagan origins. I found comfort in the fact that the dancing I loved linked with and, in some ways, both covered and incorporated the darker aspects of my life. There were powerful forces which, given the right circumstances, had the potential to attach themselves to the Morris rituals with quite devastating results. Yet, I never divulged any of this to the others. I also have a fearful respect for the figurine on the side of the church tower buttress.

*　　*　　*

The small boy had cringed in fear, mesmerised by the incessant chanting of the Machi and the pounding of the *kultrun* drum. His father, a missionary Doctor, was being forced to watch the ritual cure because his medical skills had failed to heal the hunter who had been savaged by a puma. In pigeon English, the chief of the tribe had compelled him, at spear-point, to observe the Machi's gruesome magic and manipulation of parts of the body that saved the man's life. The child shuddered at the screams of the poor creature in its death throes and the sight of blood pouring from the slit throat. The goat was sacrificed with its blood being drunk by the praying onlookers to the beating of the symbolic drum before the beast was burned to drive away the *wekulfe* spirits and extract the wounds from the hunter.

The episode had a devastating effect on the older Palfrey's subsequent career. Upon returning to England, he had continued to practise as a GP but his experience in Chile, combined with the tragic death of his beloved wife, led to his total rejection of the Christian faith, to which he had been previously so committed. His son observed his father becoming increasingly odd and disappearing frequently to congregate with what he described as his 'new-found friends'. In fact, he had also moved away from all of his old medical cronies and began to dabble with shamanistic methods of healing which, his son was to discover, sometimes involved experimenting with dark forces.

* * *

Lionel Palfrey sat in his favourite seat by the window looking out over the pond and glimpsing the church that would have once meant so much to his dad. He sipped his rum with a tear in his eye as he reflected on the father that he had always loved, who had confided some dreadful secrets to him upon his deathbed, and who had made Lionel promise to continue to explore his beliefs. He had given the young man a list of names and contacts, and made him swear to meet up with them and become involved in their activities. Although Lionel ultimately became a successful lawyer, he was determined to carry out his father's dying wishes. Moreover, following the old man's death he made that return visit to Chile. With reflections of this in his mind, he moved over to his desk and continued to write his memoirs. They were all hastily scribbled in longhand but his trustworthy secretary,

Molly, would later type all of it up on the word processor he had bought her for the office. Palfrey still preferred to write with an old-fashioned fountain pen.

Chapter 10

The first thing McQuaid noticed was the pond. It was quite large and looked serene with the church in the background. Kelvin had never experienced the charm of a relatively unspoilt, remote English village before and had a feeling that he was going to fall in love with it. Things were beginning to improve and compensate for his earlier experiences of London and Bury St Edmunds. From the little he knew about Charlotte Rossini, he gathered that she was sophisticatedly cultured and could understand why an idyllic spot such as this would be preferable to the hurly burly of Manhattan with a pig of a husband. However, his was not to reason why or question the man who was paying him handsomely. He had to remind himself that he had a job to do and needed to deliver the goods to that same ogre even though he seriously disliked him.

'Thorpe Amberley,' announced the bus driver. The farmer's wife had left the vehicle a couple of miles back with the same amount of fuss she had made when climbing aboard.

'Pretty ol' place,' she had said. 'Although there's some strange goings on at times! There's a pub called The Swan And Signet if you're looking for somewhere to stay. Does a good breakfast, but nobody drinks there. Bit mysterious. They all use The Crooked Cat.'

Before McQuaid could question her, the woman had clattered her new metallic possessions down the steps and disappeared through a rickety gate in an overgrown thorn hedge.

* * *

As he arrived at what he thought was an English rural paradise, McQuaid did not know that he was entering a maelstrom of evil. He was not to know that about a mile away, in a barn, Jamie Newman had writhed in agony with a pitchfork embedded in his abdomen and had slowly bled to death on his father's farm. His assailant had watched and cackled with hideous laughter at the distress caused before burying him alive, some distance away, and calmly driving to the pub for a pint.

* * *

'What do you know about that hideous figure on the side of one of the church tower buttresses?'

Charlotte was itching to pick Maggie Driscoll's brains about some of the local legends and mysteries, especially about Morris Dancing and all of that pagan-related stuff. Besides which she wanted to immediately use it as a diversion from any of Maggie's potential amorous advances that she suspected might materialise in due course.

'Well I'm just in it all for the crack,' Driscoll replied. 'The bloke who knows more about such things is Lionel Palfrey, but he's a bit of a weird old bugger, from snippets of conversation I've heard. Think he knows about dark arts and ritual killings and such … shouldn't worry too much about it though, the gargoyle has been there since the fourteenth century. Don't imagine it's much of a threat in the twentieth!'

* * *

One of the few regulars at The Swan And Signet found that it met his general desire to enjoy his own company. Here, he could prop up the bar and swill some lager without being told that real ale was the 'man's drink' as was the norm with the Tamberleys. He had joined them thinking that it would be good for him to socialise, but it was not working too well.

Simon Carew was pissed off being humiliated by that bastard copper. He knew he was still useless at dancing but, hell, he was still a novice and he tried hard. It was very complicated. There were seventeen Morris 'traditions' and many dances within each one. In some cases, there were variations of the same dance from one tradition to another, such as 'Constant Billy' of which there were seven different versions, some with short 'sticks' and others with long ones. Perhaps most notable were those from 'Headington', 'Adderbury' and 'Oddington' because the diverse styles had developed in these Oxfordshire and Gloucestershire villages where English Morris had its origins.

Simon still found it extremely hard to 'burn-in' the Morris Double-Step, let alone combine this with following the tracking of the dances, each of which was totally different, while simultaneously performing either the stick or handkerchief movements. Clever clogs Hetherington, who had been doing it all since childhood, could not appreciate that somebody like Carew did not take easily to performing all three of these actions at the same time and, furthermore, coordinating it all with the rest of the guys in the smooth flow of the dance. Because of his inexperience, he was commanded to spend too much time inside that fucking stoat where he could simply jump around and not spoil the rhythm of the dancing. However, this was not enabling him to develop his skills.

Added to his unhappiness at the farm, Carew's resentment towards Morris Dancing and with everything and everybody in Thorpe Amberley was gaining pace. Even a short trip home to see his estranged parents in Devon had been depressing. There was also the problem of his half-brother, the miserable bastard. There was only one immediate glimmer of light in his sorry existence and that was the prospect of meeting the new American girl.

As he sat there slurping his Carlsberg and drowning his sorrows, a stranger walked in. Another US accent. 'Surely not?' thought Carew.

Chapter 11

Carl Rossini loved money, not so much for the sake of it but for what money could buy. And Rossini loved possessions because owning things denoted power and that was what he craved more than anything. His properties in New York, the Hamptons and in far away Las Vegas were a testimony to this. Above all, he loved to own people. They were the best possessions of all. In short, he was a control freak.

Possibly, he could be forgiven, for this was the way of his family and their values that, as a child, he had not realised had been indoctrinated into him.

His beautiful wife, Charlotte, was yet another possession, albeit a very important one. She was a jewel, a gemstone to be flaunted, to be seen and to be shown off. Whores were to be fucked. She was to be owned as was the hireling, McQuaid, who was being paid a king's ransom to bring her back. Since Carl had received the news that the detective had located her, his impatience grew and he had no perception of the delicate procedures that Kelvin, the consummate professional, was going to have to engineer in order to deliver the goods to his master. He also had no knowledge of the terror which potentially threatened his wife.

*   *   *

Sarah Wilderspin had overslept partly because she was a little peeved about the potential intentions of her partner with whom she had lived and loved for five years. Maggie and

Sarah had shared their two-up, two-down terraced house on the outskirts of Thorpe Amberley and had spent much time and money on lovingly restoring it from the dilapidated state in which they purchased it, very cheaply, from a local farmer. Sarah felt rough. This was due to the consumption of half a bottle of whisky the night before in the wake of a spat with Maggie. It had become obvious that from the night Driscoll had first seen Charlotte in The Crooked Cat her lover was besotted. Whereas Sarah had become fatter through over-indulgence in chocolates, fine wine and sheer idle content-ment, Maggie had kept herself more in trim and the gorgeous American girl was a temptation that her partner could not resist. When she had told Sarah that she was taking Charlotte out to lunch to get to know her, and persuade her to join the Tambourines, they had argued. 'So I'm unattractive,' jabbed Sarah, cuttingly. 'If you say so …' Maggie had retorted with indignation at being quizzed as to whether or not she should dare to choose to go to lunch with somebody. Her freedom was being challenged and more harsh words were said as the tiff escalated into a full-blown row.

The cottage reeked of Maggie's roll-ups which was a constant annoyance to Sarah who had tried hard to quit smoking. Now, hung-over and seriously pissed off, she grabbed one of her last remaining ciggies from a crumpled packet. It was dry and fairly revolting as she inhaled the nicotine with tears rolling from swollen eyes, which had just witnessed evidence of Maggie having dolled herself up with make-up for her assignation with beauty.

'If anything develops from this, somebody will pay for it,' she mouthed to herself.

* * *

McQuaid was becoming slowly accustomed to the anachronisms that seemed to prevail in this strange land, so maybe he was not that surprised at the sound of the little bell that tinkled merrily above his head as he walked into The Swan, or whatever it was called. How quaint all of these old pub names were. After the frantic slickness of America, New York in particular, he was beginning to feel some warmth towards this old-fashioned world.

He entered a musty, beery-smelling atmosphere. An ancient clock ticked monotonously and loudly, dominating the otherwise silent room. A large tabby Bagpuss of a cat slept comfortably on top of one end of the bar. 'Gotta break all of the health regulations,' Kelvin muttered to himself. Propping up the same bar was the only customer, a thin, reclusive looking guy who hardly raised an eyebrow at his entrance. There was nobody behind the bar.

'Is anybody in charge of this place?'

'Just ring the bell,' Carew replied.

McQuaid noticed a very large hand bell next to the snoring cat. Next to the bell was a tin in which there were a few coins and a £5 note. The tin was marked 'Help yourself'.

'He's not here, mind, still out on his post round. Does quite a few jobs does our Jimmy.'

As Kelvin prepared to ask why the stranger had told him to bother to ring the bell in the first place, a wrinkled old woman appeared through the plastic, dangling multi-coloured curtains covering a door space behind the bar.

With a cigarette drooping from her mouth, she mumbled, 'Can I 'elp?'

'It's the landlord's aunt,' said Simon Carew.

* * *

Maggie Driscoll edged closer to Charlotte, as she prepared to say more about Lionel Palfrey, and saw the American's question as an opportunity to make body contact while giving an answer.

As she tried to put her hand on Charlotte's knee, the American beauty rasped, in her best Bostonian accent, 'Listen honey, let's get one thing established: I'm straight, okay, fucking straight!'

Driscoll was not prepared for such a sharp reaction from the girl that she had thought, for an American, was so genteel. She looked totally shocked and was obviously not aware that, through being married to Carl Rossini, Charlotte had also acquired a strong element of New York's streetwise behaviour.

Chapter 12

As the Learjet touched down at the airport for the gambling Mecca of the world, Carl Rossini wondered just what the hell he was doing. The control freak in him said that he should be landing some five thousand miles away to sort out his wife, now that he knew she was shacked up in some godforsaken village in rural England. It was not in his nature to trust and he was not sure that McQuaid, despite a reputation as the best in the business, would deliver the goods fast enough to satisfy his impatience. He had been all set to fly to London and then on to wherever it was she was located, when a property deal threatened to fall through. Vegas was the largest building site on the planet, where hotels and casinos were in a perpetual state of being demolished and replaced by bigger, better and glitzier structures. In this case one of the family hotels had already been knocked down and a legal wrangle had developed about the construction of its successor. Seemingly, the family had been double-crossed by a crooked lawyer. It demanded the immediate attention of their troubleshooter and bully-boy who, underneath his charming exterior that won over congressmen, had his own ruthless methods of solving problems.

As Rossini stepped off the plane and into the waiting stretch limo, he grabbed his cell phone to call McQuaid again. Later that day, the body of a Las Vegas attorney was thrown, chained to concrete, into the rapids of the Colorado River near the Hoover Dam.

* * *

'Listen, love, I've probably given you the wrong signal. You may know what we drama types are like ... we're a touchy, feely lot, always calling each other "dar-aling" and putting hands on knees and everywhere else. Yes, I fancy you like mad, but guessed you're straight. Besides which, my partner, Sarah, would slice my tongue out if she thought I was chatting up another bird. She has a wicked temper and can be most unpredictable, if crossed.'

Charlotte looked at Maggie who, having recovered from the shock of the American's outburst was trying to make amends, despite being secretly gutted at the prospect of no chance with her newly acquired friend.

'Can we start again and remain good friends?'

'Sure,' Charlotte replied, coolly. She also realised that, given the potential precariousness of her situation with a vicious bully of a husband who would doubtlessly try to track her down, she might need a friend at some time and it didn't matter if she was a dyke.

'Great,' said Maggie. 'Now I believe you were asking for further details about old Palfrey. Well, he's difficult to make out. Rumour has it that he's into so-called "dark arts" and stuff. His wife left him years ago and he lives in that big house by the church, all alone, although there are the comings and goings of some strange people. Also funny ceremonies and such apparently take place, as well as odd happenings in the woods at night. Some of the lads reckon that he uses Morris Dancing as a cover for more sinister things.'

Charlotte's eyes widened.

'Be careful with him,' added Maggie.

* * *

Donald Hetherington did not like Carew and made no bones about it. He had tried not to pick on Simon about his lack of ability to master even the basics of Morris Dancing, but could feel the seething resentment oozing out of the lad. Yet, more than this, a copper's instinct warned him that that there was something deep and sinister about this newest recruit to the Tamberleys and he feared that matters would ultimately come to a head, possibly quite dramatically. He also constantly feared that the almost psychotic temper that he tried so hard to control, for the sake of his job, would one day get the better of him.

*   *   *

McQuaid came back down to the bar after settling into his room. The chain-smoking old dear had taken him upstairs and told him to sort everything out with the landlord. Then she had disappeared. 'Crazy Brits,' he muttered to himself and recalled that a US Air Force friend of his who had been stationed in England had said that the British liked to say, 'If you like our food, try our weather,' or vice versa. It was raining like hell outside. He wondered what breakfast might be like and hoped it would not be a repeat of the standard 'full English' that the hotel had served up. Although the chances of food that was remotely American, in a basic English pub, were even more unlikely. Maybe he could ask!

The surly young man, the only customer, had apparently left. A tall, thinnish, yet wiry man stood behind the bar, stuffing letters back into his postbag. His tanned face resembled beaten leather with wrinkles hardened by many years of push-biking around the mid-Suffolk lanes and beaten into shape by the alternating ferocity of wintry snows and red-hot summers. It had also been modified by lying in ditches, with his little Jack Russell, poaching the lord of the manor's pheasants and then selling them back to his lordship, dressed and oven-ready, when the aristocrat occasionally honoured the pub with his presence for a half pint. 'Serves the rich bugger right,' he would say.

'Afternoon, squire! Couldn't deliver these bastards.' Jimmy Tusser grinned. 'Not going all the way out to these farms in this pissing weather. Get you a drink?'

'Scotch on the rocks will do,' replied Kelvin. 'And how much for the room? I might be staying for some time, depends, don't know yet.'

'Don't worry, chief, usually fifteen quid a night but we'll come to some arrangement. Special rates for Americans! Actually, there's an American lass recently come, lives in a cottage just before the forest begins on the outskirts of the village.'

'Yeah, an old guy on the bus mentioned it, but I'm Canadian, actually.' McQuaid did not want to reveal his true identity and he had decided to hang low for a while in this ramshackle pub to try and gauge the lie of the land. Hopefully, the cheery, chirpy Jimmy, in his role as postman, would be able to provide information in response to subtle questioning. 'What about breakfast?'

'Oh, great choice, missus walked out on me two years ago. Best thing that ever happened. Girlfriend's a terrific cook, anything that involves eggs! Not just yer standard fry-up.'

'Thank Christ for that,' said McQuaid, 'maybe she could do them typically American, like "over-easy".' He took a huge slug at his whisky. 'I'll have another, make it a large one!'

Chapter 13

Charlotte had not gotten round to acquiring a car and, besides which, she was a tad nervous about driving the twisty lanes of Suffolk. Even in her part of rural New England the roads were predominantly either freeways or rough tracks leading to isolated settlements.

'There are buses, but only one a day,' Maggie had told her. 'You should try the famous market bus on a Wednesday, it's an experience not to be forgotten, especially if you don't mind sharing it with livestock!'

Having decided to indulge in a Saturday shopping expedition to Bury, Charlotte had waited patiently by the bus shelter near the pond. When the old rickety, round-topped vehicle, still in service from the 1930s, arrived ten minutes late, she was amazed at the site of a contraption that emitted blue exhaust fumes and sounded as though it was spitting pistons. In the States, it would surely have been consigned to a museum. Some elderly ladies and a few giggly youngsters also clambered aboard. Charlotte learned from them that the Saturday market in Bury St Edmunds was popular for cheap clothes, bric-a-brac and vegetable produce. The cattle market was only on Wednesdays.

'There was another American aboard the bus recently,' commented the driver when he heard her accent. 'Funny, that, never had any of you lot round here before, then we get a whole army at once!' He grinned as he handed Charlotte her ticket, leaving her full of curiosity and a little apprehensive as she thought about just how ruthless her husband was.

'Could the bastard have found out where I am?' she pondered, but such thoughts were soon replaced by the delights of what she was experiencing. There was simply nothing in the States to compare with the rumbustiousness of a large-scale English country town market. Charlotte was soon wallowing in the ecstasy of rummaging through a multiplicity of colourful garments, looking for a new top.

'Manufacturers' seconds, these, luv, all best quality from Marks and Sparks,' chirped a cheery stallholder, obviously up from London, or thereabouts. She had little idea of what he was talking about but fell in love with a little white silky blouse with frills at the front. 'Just the job, if I'm going to start some socialising with this Morris lot,' she said to herself, fumbling for her purse buried at the bottom of a bulging duffel bag.

'Yep, that one looks good.'

Corin Farnsworth moved next to Charlotte. 'So you've found the famous Bury market, then?'

She blushed a little but it was comforting to see a familiar face.

'Sure, isn't it great!'

'Not coming to our performance this afternoon?' Corin continued.

Charlotte said that she didn't know anything about it. 'Besides which, I've got to catch the return bus at ...'

'Not at all,' he cut in. 'How's about I treat you to a spot of lunch and then run you straight there. I have my kit on the back of my bike, ready for the off. We're dancing at the Drinkstone Country Fair, and there's a nice pub for a drink afterwards!'

Charlotte looked at the fellow in his tartan working shirt, revealing big sun-bronzed arms. 'He's one hell of a good looking guy,' she thought.

'Bike?' she queried.

'Yeah, the only way to travel. My old BSA, British motor

bike, exhilarating but a bit breezy! Oh, and I always carry a spare helmet in one of the side panniers, should just about fit you!' He laughed.

The answer was not difficult. She was being propositioned into a kind of date, albeit involving being frozen to death, Morris Dancing and probably the rest of the Tamberleys.

'Sure,' she said that well used American word. 'Lead the way to the food, kind sir.'

* * *

A coffee-maker smashed to the kitchen floor, followed by a brick being thrown through the television screen in the adjacent sitting room. Wrecked crockery, broken lamps and splintered bits of furniture almost completed the devastation of Charlotte's cottage. The aggressive vandal was not happy. In fact she was livid. 'Take that you Yankee bitch!' she snarled, hurling a small chair into a rear window, before escaping through it and, in such a rage, not noticing that she had cut her arm on one of the bits of remaining jagged glass.

The insanely jealous Sarah had sat in her car, observing Charlotte's movements for some days, and had grabbed her opportunity when she had seen the American leave for the bus that Saturday morning. Putting masking tape on the back door window, it was easy to gently break the glass and turn the large, old metal key within to unlock it and gain entry. This would teach the fucking colonial to try and intervene.

How wrong she was.

* * *

Kelvin had struck up quite an accord with the seemingly multi-talented Jimmy and a friendship was developing. In return, the landlord of The Swan was slightly chuffed at having a Commonwealth citizen staying in his pub. 'Just love yer accent squire,' he said. 'Just where the bloody hell do you come from in Canada?' McQuaid was so tempted to say 'New York' but wanted to keep up the charade for as long as possible. Nevertheless, he hated lying to people he liked.

'Toronto,' he replied, and this is what the village would come to believe as the grapevine spread word about the newcomer. He hoped Charlotte would buy the deception as well. He did not realise that he was about to see her sooner than planned.

'Tell yer what, Mr Toronto,' the publican announced on the first Saturday of Kelvin's stay. 'How's about a little trip out later? The pub will be empty and Maisie can look after the last bit of the lunchtime bar session anyway. It's the Drinkstone Country Fair this afternoon, everybody will be going, big event every year, loads of stalls selling just about every rural product, marquees with jam to huge onions! There's also a gymkhana.'

'A what?' interrupted McQuaid.

'Horse Show to you, mate. Gymkhana's what the toffs call it, show jumping and dressage and ... well ... horses, of course.'

Kelvin didn't feel any the wiser.

'Yeah,' continued Jimmy. 'And also lot of other displays in the main ring ... oh, and by the way, our very own Morris Men, the Tamberleys, will be performing. Snobby lot of bastards apart from young Simon. They never use this pub, all frequent The Cat with its real fucking ales. But they're good to look at, very colourful and professional! I think the Tambourines, the women's lot, might be appearing as well. We'll take my old jeep if you don't mind being chucked about a bit – only joking!'

'Morris Men?' McQuaid was now totally confused. 'Yeah, sure,' he said. 'Sounds a good laugh!'

* * *

Cockfield Green, the location of the Drinkstone Country Fair, was pulsating with life. The normally placid stretch of greensward was a cacophony of sound combined with visual exuberance. As the Stowmarket Silver Band finished playing a popular medley, finishing with an out-of-tune version of the *William Tell Overture*, they were succeeded in the main roped-off arena by a girls' drum majorette marching display. There followed the somewhat irritating tingle-tingling of vertical little xylophones combined with the incessant blowing of kazoos, accompanied by off-beat drumming in a rendition of 'When The Saints Go Marching In'. Yet the huge crowd loved it all.

'What a bloody row,' shouted Corin, joking above the noise.

Charlotte smiled and squeezed his arm. It was good to be in the company of a real man again, with, so far, no sign of the Tamberleys. 'They're only kids,' she laughed. 'Give them a chance. When are you lot on?'

'Oh, they'll all be arriving in dribs and drabs soon, about an hour from now. Some of them will be late as usual.'

On the far side of the Green, having been directed by stewards wearing yellow plastic body warmers, McQuaid clambered out of Jimmy's ancient jeep, much shaken after the bumpiest ride of this life. 'Is a slipped disc an optional extra?' he had taunted the publican. Kelvin had never witnessed anything quite like the scene before him. 'Crazy Brits,' he said to himself, although maybe it compared a little to the ebullience of a small-town rodeo he had once witnessed when on holiday in Williams, Arizona, after flying over the Grand Canyon. 'Maybe not, though,' he reflected.

His thoughts were interrupted as Jimmy shouted to him when the majorettes marched noisily off.

'There's the young lady from your side of the pond,' yelled

Jimmy as the passing kazoos blasted their eardrums. 'Over there.' He pointed. 'Charlotte, they call her, comes from somewhere around New York, doesn't drink in my pub, though, hangs out with the Tamberley elite at The Cat.'

Kelvin stared across at the gorgeous creature on the arm of a brawny, lumberjack of a guy. She was dressed casually in skin-tight jeans tucked into expensive brown leather boots which matched her long, lightweight beige leather coat.

'Who's the boyfriend ?'

'Oh, that's Corin Farnsworth, also one of the Morris Dancers. Used to teach, I believe, now works with rehabilitating hooligans in the forest. Also has a cottage in the middle of it which apparently goes with the job. Convenient if they're getting it together, their two cottages are not that far apart!'

'Yep,' McQuaid said to himself, looking at Mrs Rossini's immaculate clothes. 'Bit like my ex-wife. This dame sure knows how to spend Carl's money.' At last, he had found his target and was staring at the reality of the situation. 'Take it from here, buddy,' he whispered to himself as he reached for his cell phone. 'Better update the bastard, I suppose. He won't like it though!'

Chapter 14

As Charlotte had left to catch the bus, she was followed. As she waited at the shelter, the same eyes that had previously watched her depart with Maggie Driscoll a week earlier burned with intensity from within the bushes at the side of the pond. The mouth below them salivated as the tongue swept around its lips. When the bus was underway, an old farm Land Rover chugged along in its wake. As the young American woman alighted near the Bury market, the driver parked up in a nearby back street but soon managed to spot the beauty, in a long leather coat, amongst the crowded shoppers. He saw her meet up with Farnsworth, whom he had begun to regard as something of a friend, and felt betrayed. A violent inner rage welled up inside him.

* * *

As the Learjet took off from Vegas, Carl received a text message from McQuaid.

> *Found your wife. Situation complex. Proceeding with caution. Patience needed. Will keep you informed. McQuaid.*

The problem was that Rossini was not a patient man. He moved up to sit behind his pilot. 'Put this fucking kite into top gear,' he said. 'I might want you to fly on to England … New York first, refuel and take it from there. I'll reassess the situation then.'

*   *   *

On Cockfield Green, there was all the fun of the fair. At the far end there were some rides, inflatables and such for the kids; just a little carousel and swings, a coconut shy and a darts stall with prizes. In the main ring, the small parade of cattle came and went with a huge white champion Charolais bull defecating all over the field.

'There's no way we're going to dance in cowshit,' Lionel Palfrey had told the organiser, after he had seen the problem. They hurriedly roped off a clean area for the Tamberleys to perform. 'And make sure it's smooth,' Donald Hetherington had added. 'We can break ankles on rough surfaces.'

At three o'clock, the unique sounding drum and tabor struck up from somewhere behind the field and Morris men dramatically danced through a gap in the crowd, with their leg bells ringing, to rapturous applause.

Simon Carew had looked on and wondered which poor sod amongst them was sweating inside the stoat. It should have been him, but he had told them he had to work. They did not see him high up inside the Land Rover, parked out of sight, with binoculars. Sweeping around the field, he saw them. He also saw Charlotte, with her arms around Corin Farnsworth, developing into a clinch and then a kiss. How the relationship had rapidly moved on!

In the other direction, he thought he spotted the Canadian guy who appeared to be looking towards the new lovebirds.

The Tamberleys immediately burst into their opening routine of the famous 'Adderbury', 'Lads A Buncham', with its rousing song of *'Oh dear mother what a fool I've been'*. Charlotte stood alone, by the field rope, trying to spot Corin in the rapid tracking of the dance amidst the clashing of sticks, swirling of ribbons and intermittent jumping up and down of straw hats, all in a kaleidoscope of complicated, multicoloured movement.

'I've heard that song before.' She remembered her first encounter with it when passing the Village Hall. 'However do they do it?' she asked herself in admiration and wonder.

The performance continued with a series of dances from many of the different traditions, alternating between either short or long sticks or just white handkerchiefs alone. The highlight was the aggressive fighting dance, always an audience pleaser, of 'The Vandals of Hammerwich' from the slightly rarer Midlands 'Lichfield' tradition. The sticks were clashed with such violent force that this 'party piece' invariably featured lumps of wood flying off into the crowd like a cricket ball hit for a six at a test match. The quite spectacular finale was when they danced off in a line towards, around and through the onlookers, singing the traditional 'Bonny Green Garters'.

'Now here's to the ladies, we love them so well,
Even though they are tartars.
So off with their stockings and off with their shoes
And off with their Bonny Green Garters ... '

The crowd loved it.

Also clapping her hands with glee, Charlotte was aware of somebody sidling up to her. 'You're from Am-Am-merica, aren't you?'

As she turned to face the speaker, Corin, having broken away from the rest, came striding across.

'Hello, Simon,' he interrupted, 'thought you were supposed to be at work!'

'Not supposed to be here, going back now, keep it to yourself,' Carew snarled with indignation. He stormed off before Corin could introduce him to Charlotte. However, he had seen, close up, what he wanted to see, and his face was thunderous.

*   *   *

DCI 'Willy' Williams came out of the forensic lab, deep in the basement below the complex of Exeter nick.

'Yep,' he told his team. 'The body was buried alive all right and the doc in there has worked out, from dental records, that the poor bastard's name is Andrew Carew. Lived with his old mum at Widecombe in the Moor. The forensic team are all interested in the butt of what could either be a cigarette or a joint. It's under the microscope right now. They're trying to work upon some kind of DNA analysis.'

Chapter 15

As they walked arm in arm across the Green to Farnsworth's bike, a somewhat piqued Lionel Palfrey had watched them go. Corin took Charlotte to one of his favourite, romantic haunts, a huge thatched inn near Bury St Edmunds which was famed for its steaks and traditional English fare.

'I don't suppose steak and kidney pudding appeals on a summer's evening,' laughed Corin. 'Lovely on a wintry night, though. However, they do a mean T-bone; think they're barbequing in the garden, round the back. Smells great and the real ale is bloody good here, too.'

In a marquee on the velvety lawn a jazz band was playing slow, swinging, quite romantic stuff. It reminded Charlotte of the States except that this was all so very English with the scent of honeysuckle and people supping pints out of big dimple-jug glasses, filled from a traditional wooden barrel. 'Chicken'll do fine,' she laughed as Corin apologised that all the steak had been eaten and that the other alternatives were bangers and burgers. 'Bangers?' she had queried.

They took their paper plates, bulging with salad and poultry bits, to a secluded picnic table by the little brook that ran by the side of the pub.

'So ... why did the Tambourines not appear today?' Charlotte asked.

'Dunno,' replied Corin. 'Like us, sometimes, they probably had trouble getting enough dancers to turn up.'

'And who was that unpleasant little guy who started to talk to me as you came across, and then, very rudely, left in a huff?'

'Yeah, he's a sad bloke. Simon Carew. Fairly new to the side, comes from Devon and works on a farm, which he hates. Think he joined the Tamberleys to make some friends but he doesn't fit in very well and particularly has friction with Don Hetherington, our Foreman. I feel sorry for him really and have tried to help, but he rejects friendship and, as you saw, can be very offhand or downright bloody rude. Bit of a weirdo really.'

Raising her eyebrows, with a face showing pity, and shrugging her shoulders, Charlotte continued sipping her pint. 'Aren't I decadent?' she said, putting the mug down and taking Corin's hand. 'Come back to my cottage and take me to bed.'

* * *

Back at The Swan, McQuaid was quite animated. The pub was officially shut.

'I'll have another large scotch,' he said. 'And another one for you, Jimmy!'

'You trying to get me drunk? I've got to open up again in two hours. Haven't even had me tea yet and I can't ask Maisie to do the honours again, she's still slightly got the hump over me being out all afternoon.'

'Just one for the road, then, just to say thanks for a wonderful afternoon. Morris Dancing, eh? Can't work out whether or not those guys are crazy or just plain brilliant, there's certainly nothing like it in …'

Kelvin stopped short. He'd almost said 'New York'.

Coughing a lot, he spluttered, 'T-Toronto.'

Jimmy seemed to recognise the slight hesitation and realised he had never asked a significant question.

'What exactly do you do for a living in Canada?'

McQuaid was prepared for this. 'I'm actually in the Royal Canadian Mounted Police.'

'Bloody 'ell, an actual Mountie! Put it there, squire!' Jimmy enthused, holding out his hand. 'Shake it ... wait till I tell the lads! Eh, there's a copper in that Morris lot you saw this afternoon, name's Hetherington, reckon you'll have a bundle in common but you'll need to catch him in the pub up the road. Not that I'm trying to lose business, mind!' He winked.

*　*　*

'You've done what?!' Maggie Driscoll stormed in an uncharacteristic rage. She had been out checking around other members of the Tambourines as to whether or not there would be enough of them available to perform that afternoon. It was a common problem trying to get a side together during the summer months and the school holidays when a number of the women, especially those with kids, were committed to being away on holiday. Maggie also favoured the personal touch, wherever possible, as opposed to the telephone, and liked to offer help to busy mums if any costumes or equipment needed sorting out. This enhanced loyalty by promoting bonding amongst the group, helping to create camaraderie and keep everybody together in the face of so many other diversions. Maggie knew that if members became discontented and left, then the Tambourine side would fall apart and ultimately die.

Tired after driving around and just about managing to get a scratch side together for the Drinkstone Country Fair she had arrived home just before midday, with barely enough time to get ready herself and swallow a quick Pot Noodle lunch. Maggie was devastated to find Sarah, on the floor, clutching the dregs of a bottle of vodka, pissed as a fart and possibly in need of medical attention.

I've ... I've ... s-smash ... smashed ... Yanks' f-f-fuck-fucking cottage!' she sputtered before puking on the floor, dropping the bottle and passing out.

Maggie was beset with a mixture of fury and fear. Clearly, the stupid bitch would, at the very least, need her stomach pumped and probably a visit to the West Suffolk Hospital in Bury. 'You silly cow!' she raged over the comatose body on the floor. Yet her teacher's instincts and experience of dealing with emergencies in schools over the years quickly brought her to take swift damage-limitation action. She wiped the vomit away from Sarah's lips and gave mouth to mouth resuscitation until normal breathing was restored. 'Ambulance next,' she chivvied herself, grabbing her mobile. After connecting with the medics and waiting for them to arrive, she began to phone all of the Tambourines and systematically undo all her efforts of the morning. Thank God they were understanding. Even so, cancelling at the last moment could have long-term repercussions for the future.

She held Sarah in her arms. 'Fuck you,' she said as her partner began to groan again in between nodding off and waking. 'I've had to call off our performance. Just as well I suppose that I love you, otherwise I should have bloody well let you choke to death!'

'S-so … sorry,' moaned Sarah, before lapsing into sleep again as a blue light flashed outside the door.

* * *

Charlotte loved her little cottage and approaching it along the small winding gravel path, with her arm linked around a most desirable hunk, charged her with a mixture of emotion and intense sexual arousal. She had not been fucked for a few years, save for a brief assignation with a boring fart in Winchester; a friend of her parents. He had taken advantage of her after one of those tedious, twee, very Ivy League dinner parties when she had imbibed far too much expensive wine. It had been a disaster. His prick had been flaccid and he had fallen asleep before even finishing the job that he had barely started. Neither could she remotely evoke any recollection of when she had last been screwed by Carl. At the front door, Corin took her in his arms and kissed her so passionately that her hormones accelerated into overdrive.

Yet horror was to follow. As they entered the cottage, full of pent up lust for each other, their eyes met a scene of total devastation. Charlotte simply burst into floods of tears.

In a state of disbelief, they were unaware of the front door closing and failed to notice who was staring at them through the window from behind the trees in the garden.

Chapter 16

Rossini received McQuaid's call back in New York. He was already tired and irritable from the trip to Vegas and the Learjet had hit severe turbulence on the return journey, especially avoiding tornado 'twisters' in the mid-West. His mood, tinged with a little delight that McQuaid had found the bitch, was nonetheless made more savage by the knowledge that Charlotte was possibly dating another guy. Nobody took away his possessions and as such he would take no prisoners, as the Vegas attorney had discovered when he was hurled alive into the swirling waters of the Colorado.

Georgio was gay and totally loyal to his demanding taskmaster. Rossini accepted his sexuality because the Italian was both highly efficient and ruthless when need be. In his main homosexual relationship, Georgio was the butch one and was in the process of shafting his lover when the phone rang. 'Shit, the boss wants me, and that means now!' he exclaimed, withdrawing from the performance, leaving his partner panting and frustrated.

Rossini yelled into the mouthpiece. 'Georgio! Stop fucking, get the hell over here and start making preparations. We're going to little old England!'

* * *

Back home, Palfrey was a tad miffed. Farnsworth had obviously scored, or was about to. 'Bloody shame,' he said to himself, 'especially when I was the one who first met

83

Charlotte and persuaded her to get involved with the Tamberleys.' Maybe it was a matter of his age. He poured himself a large Jamaica rum, took off the tabard of his Morris kit and fumbled with the small silver pagan effigy that hung around his neck, on a chain, beneath his white shirt.

*   *   *

Farnsworth's first reaction was to look out of the window. Some vibe, maybe associated with his ex-teacher's sixth sense of an impending problem, told him that there was something he had seen in the corner of his eye when they had neared the cottage. He thought he had glimpsed a Land Rover accelerating up the lane. Yet he was a mixture of emotions from the shock of what had happened to the beginning of an erection building up in his anticipation and longing to make passionate love to the stunningly beautiful creature before him who eagerly felt the same way.

Charlotte was sobbing as she now clung to him, the wetness of her face and long blonde hair soaking the front of his shirt. His erection stiffened even more. 'Fuck it,' he blurted, tenderly pulling her towards the stairs, only stopping to kiss her passionately as they entered the bedroom where the intruder had not ventured. 'I'll clear this up later, I've a reasonable idea of who's the culprit and I'll get Don Hetherington to unofficially sort it.'

'Ssh ...' Charlotte moaned as she ripped off her dress, felt the protrusion in his jeans and began to unbutton the top of them.

*   *   *

McQuaid was enjoying an unaccustomed late afternoon nap following a few too many glasses of scotch. 'Silly bugger,' he had scolded himself before lying down. His crafty snooze was

84

interrupted by the staccato jabbing of the ringtone from his cell phone.

'Shit!' was his reaction as he reached for the annoying little appliance that seemed to control his life.

A strong New York accent assaulted his eardrum.

'Get your ass into gear, I'm on my way!' Rossini's unmistakeable voice bellowed at him.

'Shit!', he repeated. He had a slightly thumping headache. 'Only one thing for it, sonny,' he said to himself. 'Quick shower and shave, change of clothes something to eat and hair of the dog. About time I looked in at the other pub!'

*   *   *

Georgio was multi-talented guy. Apart from being a highly efficient secretary with a typing speed of a hundred words a minute and a competent organiser, he was also a qualified pilot and, as an ex-special forces officer, a trained, ruthless killer and assassin. He was simply the best, which is why he was paid a fortune by Rossini and owned a luxury villa in his beloved Sicily. However, the boss would not be too pleased when he told him that the Learjet had developed some technical faults during the battering it had taken in ducking and diving through the turbulence on the return from Las Vegas.

'It's being worked on right now,' he had told Rossini. 'Should be done in a couple of days, the alternative is flying commercial.'

'Fuck that,' Carl had screamed, incandescent with rage. 'Get it sorted, or your job's on the line!' He did not mean it, of course. 'And get your weaponry ready. You need to be tooled up for this one!'

*   *   *

Despite the initial problem of the grass location for the dancing, it had been a most successful afternoon. Hetherington allowed himself the luxury of an early evening drink in The Cat. He was happily supping his beer when a seemingly North American accent announced, without subtlety, 'I'll have pint of what he's having.'

Being a total Anglophile and not too fond of his American cousins, the countrified copper was a shade irate at his reverie being so interrupted.

'You Yanks have got a bloody cheek,' he sneered.

'Canadian, actually,' McQuaid retorted as he held out his hand. 'Kelvin McQuaid, detective in the Royal Canadian Mounted Police.'

Instantly, Hetherington's attitude changed. With a broad smile, he warmly grabbed McQuaid's hand. 'Well that makes it different! 'I'm a policeman, myself. Get this man a pint of Black Dog,' he requested the landlord.

As the jovial John Harrison lovingly poured a measure of the renowned real ale, McQuaid asked if, by any chance, his new-found friend was Donald Hetherington.

'The very same,' said Donald.

Harrison passed the foaming jug across the bar. 'You'll never want to drink anything else,' he chirped.

Before they could continue the pleasantries, Hetherington's mobile burst into the 'Mexican Hat Dance', it's somewhat annoying ringtone. Corin Farnsworth was on the line.

Chapter 17

Jimmy Tusser did not always put undelivered letters back into the post box unless, of course, he was still drunk from the night before. The Swan had a reputation for both heavy drinking and its roughneck clientele.

Mostly, he was up like a lark and conscientious. His sharp poacher's eyes did not miss a thing and he could spot a hare half a mile away.

He was horribly surprised to see a pair of boots sticking out of a muddy bank. It had rained heavily for two days and his early morning delivery had been a misery. He knew the boots, instantly – they belonged to an ex-customer who he had fallen out with and banned from The Swan. Jake Newman now only occasionally frequented The Cat.

*   *   *

To most people, wading about in cow dung on a Saturday afternoon would be a less than wonderful experience. Yet, as Simon Carew splashed about in his wellies through the relatively liquid, foul substance, it was manna from heaven.

'There you go my beauties!' He stroked Lulu Belle's arse as he hosed the shit from the cows' rumps. 'Soon get you all tucked up in your nice cosy barn. Good job old Simon looks after you ain't it?'

He was happier now, away from the poncey country fair where, despite the Morris Dancing, he did not feel that he fitted in. It was good to be back at the farm, tending to his beloved beasts, especially as the vile Newmans were no longer around.

* * *

Lionel Palfrey had no love for most of the farmers of Thorpe Amberley. Despite their appearances of being ruddy-faced stereotypes of jovial rurality, mostly they were a macho crowd, full of withering testosterone and renowned for their daily, mammoth consumption of beer. It was quite common for some of them to enter the pub at lunchtime and stay there until at least the early evening. Admittedly, most of them were up at the crack of dawn with an early start on their farms and by midday had probably earned their relaxation but, generally, they were a jaundiced lot who thought that nobody else ever did any real work and that the rest of the world owed them a living. Save for Edwin Garner and his few cronies, thank God, most of them, including the despicable Newmans, no longer drank in The Cat, from where they had either been barred or had simply chosen to frequent The Swan instead. Here, their crude swearing and raucous rudeness was tolerated by the postman oaf of a landlord. Garner was best described as a pain in the arse but his frequent insults towards Palfrey and the Tamberleys were tolerable if ignored. The worst of the offenders had been the Newmans, who made poor Simon Carew's life hell. Palfrey had often thought that if murder was legal he could easily use his knowledge to kill both Jake and his horrible son. He poured himself another drink and habitually rubbed the small effigy around his neck.

* * *

Maggie had not fully recovered from the events of the day before. Sarah had more or less recuperated from her total stupidity, yet Maggie was still in a mixed state of love, anger and pain. Having phoned Charlotte to tell her about Sarah's stupidity, apologising profusely, she felt the need for a long country walk to clear her head and sort her emotions out. Charlotte had said, 'Corin Farnsworth is helping me to clear up the mess. We're becoming a bit of an item – I told you I was straight!' Charlotte had laughed and hung up.

As Driscoll neared Jake Newman's farm, something made her look again at what she had first thought to be a withering clump of brown tussock grass protruding from the deep ditch at the side of the road. Upon closer inspection, she let out a scream of abject horror. It was human hair, beneath which was the glimpse of a head.

* * *

Hetherington was just about to explain to McQuaid that he needed to do a friend a favour when Farnsworth phoned him again to explain that they now knew who had trashed the cottage and that the matter was being sorted.

Hetherington briefly explained it to McQuaid. 'The joys of being a copper in a village,' he laughed.

'This calls for another drink,' replied Kelvin as the two policemen began to swap notes on their different styles of work.

Just as they were getting to know each other, the postman burst through the door of the pub.

'Hey! You've got the wrong pub, Jimmy!' McQuaid quipped. 'I'm slumming it in this one,' he began to say, but stopped short when he saw the horror on Tusser's face.

'Donald, I think you had better come with me … I've found Jake Newman, dead. It ain't a pretty sight. It'll be one for your big detective boys from Ipswich, but you had better start the ball rolling.'

Hetherington turned to McQuaid. 'Want to do a bit of

unofficial detective work? It'll be a couple of hours before the Regional Crime Squad arrive from our Martlesham HQ.'

As they came out of The Cat, a hysterical Maggie Driscoll rushed towards them. 'Thank God I've found you Donald, there's a human head and probably a body beneath it buried at the side of a lane … and …' she broke down in a swathe of anguish.

'Jesus Christ, said Hetherington. 'Two at the same time! I'm glad you're here, a fellow policeman, at least you can maybe give me some support until the experts arrive. The shit is about to hit the fan, national press, TV coverage, the lot!' He grabbed his mobile and tapped out a special hotline number.

Chapter 18

'Who the fuck calls a place Bury St Edmunds?'

Carl Rossini was experiencing a mixture of continued annoyance blended with some mild amusement at what he perceived to be the absurdity of British cultural history. Aside from having once touched down at Heathrow, after concluding a 'family' business deal with the Russian under-world, en route from Moscow to New York, he had never visited the UK before and much less did he care to. Now he found himself at Heathrow again wondering just how the hell he was going to get to this godforsaken place in the wilds of Sufuck, east fucking somewhere.

'Get used to it,' said Georgio, who had experienced some military service in Britain. 'We have two choices,' continued the Italian. 'I can either fly the Lear on to Cambridge airport and then on to Bury by train or we can travel all the way there by rail. In every scenario there will have to be some travel by various forms of public transport or hire car or taxi, especially to reach this remote village of Thorpe Amberley.'

'There you go again, another screwball name from the fucking Dark Ages. What a shit little country!'

'Actually, it's quite delightful.' Georgio had fond summer memories of village pubs, cricket and, despite being gay, buxom English girls in revealing low-cut floral dresses.

'Just cut the crap and get me there will yer!'

* * *

'I could do with a shower!' Charlotte looked provocatively at Corin.

'Together,' he replied with a wink. They gulped down the red wine they had poured out after the first sensational shag.

Moments later, they were scrubbing each other down with a monstrous loofah which also served as part of erotic foreplay. As the water trickled over their wet bodies, the temptations were too great and they were unable to keep their hands off each other, rubbing shower gel all over their erogenous zones in lovemaking that was fast, furious and pure lust. The shower was next to a frosted glass window which faced the front of the cottage.

Across the road, a pair of eyes watched as the pinkish-white naked forms could be seen, through the glass, writhing about in sheer ecstasy.

'But not for long, Mr Farnsworth,' muttered a voice.

* * *

'You're not joking are you Donald?'

The Head of Uniform Branch sat at his desk almost mesmerised as the full horror of what one of his most promising young coppers had just told him began to sink in. It could be the work of a serial killer and maybe potential mass murder. Who knew what further gruesome discoveries might be unearthed?

'Look, do what you can until the Crime Squad hot shots and forensic arrive. This is so serious, I imagine the Head of CID himself will personally take charge. I think the chopper will be justified to get them there within the hour. For Christ's sake get the whole bloody lot roped off to preserve whatever evidence might be at the two respective scenes … yes I know you're on your own in the middle of nowhere and it's getting dark and pissing with rain … and … what did you say? There's a visiting Canadian Mountie with you? Great, get the bugger to help. Thank God night's falling, for God's sake keep the news contained. Don't let *anybody* else know. Tell that bloody postman and drama teacher to keep their gobs shut, last thing we want is for this to reach the ears of the media until we have clearer ideas about what's happened. And get full statements from both!'

'It's not going to be easy, sir.'

'Well, it won't do your promotion chances any harm. Doesn't come any bigger than this … yes, I know you're officially off duty but you could become a hero. Take charge for now, I'll see if I can get a local squad car over there to help. Christ, I don't even know if our small force can handle it all. Might have to bring in other forces, even the bloody Met! Just wait till the national press get hold of it, but we must keep those bastards out of it for now! I'll be in touch, good luck.'

* * *

Corin was feeling pretty good. Despite the trashing of Charlotte's cottage, which they had managed to put straight again, he had had a great day and was in love. The American beauty was too good to be true and had said she now felt ready for an early night. He would have stayed but he needed to go back to his own pad for the usual crack-of-dawn start to get to the forest.

Tingling all over from their wonderful lovemaking, Charlotte watched him roar off. When he disappeared around the first bend she thought she saw a large black dog bounding after his motorbike. Still a little heady, she vaguely remembered the story Palfrey had first told her in the pub. 'Cannot be,' she scolded herself, 'must have had too much wine. To hell with it, I need another drink!'

As he rode his faithful BSA along the dark, lonely, wet road through pine woods, Corin took extra care because of the threat of skidding and falling from the old motor cycle, the other love of his life. With the pouring rain driving into the visor around his face, he could not fail to look up and see the most unexpected sight of the bright lights of a helicopter swooping low over the trees, the excessive noise of it drowning out the throaty purring of his bike engine.

'What the hell!' he began to say as the whirling monster caused him to momentarily swerve dangerously. As he did so, the headlights of a vehicle blinded him head on and combined with the rain and the chopper, the triple distraction caused the bike to topple and he found himself sprawled across the bracken by the side of the road as the old machine slid into a ditch.

A vehicle was parked in a lay-by at the side of the road, facing the oncoming traffic, its headlights were switched on, blasting strong light illegally towards any passing traffic. In a state of semi-consciousness, Farnsworth thought he had received a severe blow to the head. He was vaguely aware of a human shape standing over him and thought he recognised it. Some form of liquid was being forced into his mouth. Before his eyes closed again he thought the figure was holding something that resembled a spade and was also aware of severe pains shooting through his body from the area of his stomach. As he began to drift off, his last recollection was the howl of a large dog.

* * *

'So that's fucking Cambridge.'

'That's King's down there,' announced Georgio with enthusiasm and reverence for the magnificence of the holy opulence of the famous landmark chapel. Rossini had to admit that he was impressed at the sight of the colleges as dusk began to fall over the University, revealing a magical myriad of twinkling lights emanating from their medieval splendour. The Learjet swooped over the Cam en route to the small airport on the fringes of the city. They finally clambered out of the small plane and jumped into an extremely expensive Aston Martin which the ever efficient Italian had radioed ahead to book, having discovered the details of a local hire firm from the WAP internet facility on his 3G mobile. Money was no object.

'Beautiful though it is ... let's get the hell out of here and find this Farnsworth bastard, I want him taken out, now! Nobody steals my woman.'

Rossini was manic and forcibly extracted the details of the likely whereabouts of Corin Farnsworth from a somewhat reluctant McQuaid. 'I don't care how nice a bloke he may be,' Carl had snarled down the receiver. 'Don't forget who's paying you a ton to sort all of this out – he gets wasted!'

McQuaid again thought about his future, back in the Big Apple, with Magda. With a heavy heart and a sigh, he told his paymaster that Farnsworth was probably either at his place or at the cottage rented by Charlotte, both of which were in the vicinity of the wide forested area to the west of Thorpe Amberley. He gave Rossini the precise directions.

Georgio soon forgot to wax poetically about the historic treasures of England and put his foot down. The powerful car they had hired sped through the countryside towards Thorpe Amberley. It was now totally dark as they entered a forested stretch, but Georgio felt they were getting near. He slowed and swung the vehicle around in what appeared to be the entrance to some kind of gravel track, stopped and looked at a road map as the headlights blazed through the trees.

* * *

Hetherington and McQuaid wasted no time. They borrowed a powerful flashlight from John Harrison who shut The Cat and insisted on coming with them as the two off-duty policemen piled into Jimmy Tusser's jeep. Harrison was to follow on in his own car. Maggie Driscoll was too upset to tag along but remained behind at the pub in the company of Maisie and a large stiff whisky. She had described in detail where the gruesome head was to be found. It was chucking it down with torrential rain, dark and cold for the time of year.

Tusser guided them to where the body of Jake Newman was located and parked the jeep about fifty yards away. He grabbed some rope that he always kept in the vehicle for towing purposes.

'Don't touch a bloody thing,' Hetherington barked at the others and, having identified the body, which was already giving off a pungent smell, he asked McQuaid if he and Jimmy could rope off the road and keep guard, generally, until the Crime Squad and forensic arrived. 'So glad you're around,' he said to Kelvin. 'Makes a big difference having another professional here until the experts come.'

The second body was located a few twisty turns down an interconnecting lane and Donald requested John Harrison to drive him there to perform the same roping off and guarding procedure, while asking McQuaid to guard the first body. 'This is all we can do,' he instructed, and thanked Harrison warmly for his help. Fortunately, the landlord of The Cat also had a length of tow rope in the boot which they managed to tie around some adjacent trees. The second burial was arguably the more macabre; no wonder Driscoll hadn't wanted to return. The head had been struck across the forehead with some kind of implement, probably a spade, and congealed blood had seeped from the wound. Like the body of his father, Jamie Newman's corpse was also beginning to smell because prior to the onset of this chilly wet summer's evening the weather had been hot and close. Flies were still sticking to the blood. Hetherington noticed a small silver chain and peculiar pendant sticking out of the ground. Unlike the policeman, who was used to messy dead bodies, Harrison was not, and began to feel quite ill. He suddenly dashed across the lane and threw up into the ditch.

'Sorry about that,' he was in the process of saying when the sudden noise of a helicopter announced the arrival of the team from Suffolk Constabulary HQ. The chopper swooped around with its quite terrifying blue searchlight sweeping the terrain, not sure quite where to land. Hetherington waved at it with the beam of light from Harrison's torch. It found a small field some distance away and dropped down, the powerful rotor blades sending huge gusts of wind to shake the surrounding trees. Finally, the machine came to rest and Detective Chief Superintendent Ivor Thomas, Head of CID, clambered out.

Chapter 19

The extremely bright lights of the Aston Martin shone like searchlights through the dark, forested road. According to McQuaid, this was the area in which both Charlotte and Farnsworth resided. As the performance car gunned around a corner emitting a throaty roar, the bright light picked out a male figure who appeared to be standing over a hump by the side of the road. The sudden thrust of the engine obviously startled the man who jumped and dropped what appeared to be a long-handled implement while stepping onto the road. Georgio cursed as he swerved to avoid killing the guy. As he passed, a glance in his rear-view mirror told him that the person had run off into the trees.

'For fuck's sake Georgio!'

'Sorry boss, he came from nowhere. Looked like the asshole was about to bury something. Did you see that hump by the road? Bit suspicious, huh?'

'None of our goddamn business, what some fucked-up Brit nutcase wants to do in the middle of nowhere in the pitch dark.'

Rossini took out his cell phone and called McQuaid again.

*　*　*

'Hetherington?' Thomas held out his hand. 'Never met you before, so …' Thomas was about to congratulate his PC when a strong North American accent said, 'No sir, Donald is around the corner of the next lane with the second body.'

'Of course, you must be the Mountie. Thanks so much for helping out, we're not quite used to such activity in sleepy old Suffolk and … '

'McQuaid's the name,' Kelvin began to say but was interrupted by the ringing of his mobile. Rossini was on the line.

'Where the fuck do these two actually live in this godforsaken bloody forest? What d'you mean you can't talk now? You're with the British police? What the fuck d'you mean, dead bodies? You're working for *me*, you're not supposed to be playing Sherlock bloody Holmes!'

McQuaid turned the phone off. As he had obviously upset Rossini, he could see his fortune disappearing; but what the heck, it was good to be doing some real police work again. Hetherington and these British coppers were such cordial guys, and his conscience told him he was doing the right thing by helping to solve some brutal murders. In his heart of hearts he knew Rossini was an absolute bastard, and was it worth being held to ransom by this Mafia-connected bully boy? The turning point in his thinking was Rossini's hell bent intention to execute Farnsworth, who, from what he had gathered, seemed to be a thoroughly decent guy. If he and Charlotte could get it together and find happiness, why should he play a part in their destruction? Besides which, nothing was certain about the future of his relationship with Magda. He knew she was really a good-time girl and they had not even been in contact by phone since he had departed from the States. Having experienced the astonishing delights of this old-fashioned land and being involved with the British Police … who knew what the future might hold? Basically, he was falling in love with the Brits and their slightly quirky rural way of life. Did he really want to go back to New York? Maybe Rossini could just go to hell. Kelvin wanted no further part in his hateful schemes.

* * *

'Sorry,' he said to DCS Thomas. 'Personal call from Canada!'

Thomas made no comment and concentrated on the business in hand. 'Get me a bloody umbrella!' he yelled at his Sergeant above the receding din of the chopper blades.

'The body is over here, sir,' said McQuaid. 'Oh, this is Jimmy Tusser, by the way, local postman and publican, he found it.'

Again, Thomas made no comment but simply nodded towards Jimmy as his gimlet eye immediately directed itself towards something shiny, even in the darkness and rain, which was attached to the left boot that protruded out of the muddy bank.

His small team of highly efficient detectives were following every move, always hoping to garner the Chief Super's approval with the ever-present hope of promotion in mind. An enthusiastic young Detective Constable, Andy Perkins, immediately produced a pair of white surgical gloves and handed them to his boss. Putting the gloves on, Thomas then touched the little silver chain and strange charm.

'Looks like the clever bastard who committed this murder has attached this thing to the bloody bootlace ... and keep that brolly over me! I'm fucking soaked.'

Thomas was a big man with brainpower to match. Part of his successful rise to the top had been the possession of a photographic memory for minutiae. He now recalled recent details that he had seen, while surfing the national police database, of a similar set of circumstances pertaining to the discovery of a body on Dartmoor. And, of course, it had also been briefly featured on *Crimewatch*, although the grisly case was, as yet, far from being solved.

'The same type of bloody pendant,' he muttered to himself. 'Get me in touch with the Devon and Cornwall Police HQ, now!' Perkins approached him, wearing a pair of surgical gloves. He had a small object between the index finger and thumb of his right hand. 'Don't know if this is of any interest, sir.' The young DC showed Thomas what appeared to be the butt of a roll-up cigarette.

*   *   *

Lionel Palfrey had also heard the chopper, which was a rare occurrence in the depths of rural Suffolk at night. The unusual powers that he possessed had indicated that there had been evil afoot for some weeks now. High in the Chilean forests, the Machi, aware of problems facing her younger British protégé, was engaged in a prolonged magic ceremony of monotonous chanting along with the playing of the *kultrun*, which summed up both cosmic and earthy components. These could transcend into the supernatural world with the ordering of all beings, both material and non-material, throughout the universe. They could, thus, communicate through time and space, connecting with those who had the knowledge and power to receive. The Machi herself would remain forever inside the *kultrun*, the wooden part of which was divided into four cardinal points with the South and East being related to good while the North and West symbolised evil.

Lionel was not totally convinced of his shamanistic powers, having never had the occasion to put them to the test. Yet, unmistakably, being some 10,000 miles away, he heard the call. Sitting comfortably by his log fire, listening to Beethoven's Moonlight Sonata, he became aware of an intruding sound. Low at first, the slow beating of a drum interrupted the haunting piano air and steadily increased in intensity so that Lionel removed his headphones, wondering if there was a fault in his expensive sound system. Yet, as he did so, the noise became almost unbearable and he realised it was inside his head, and he was transported to another fire within the high forests of Patagonia. The Machi called.

As a solicitor, he was often in contact with the Police and there was certainly something amiss for the helicopter to be about. He knew where some of the problems lay and that they were being dealt with, but the control of the Machi was directing him to drive out along the forest road. He felt thus impelled to leave his cosy house and fireside chair on this chilly, wet, windy summer's evening. Reluctantly, he put down his unfinished glass of finest quality Jamaican rum, to which he was especially partial, and donned his wax Barbour jacket, leather boots and deerstalker. A dominant force drove him and his Land Rover out of the village until he came across a hump lying in the bracken at the side of the road. The hump moaned at his approach. There was a horrible gash to the head out of which blood was oozing and a spade had been dropped nearby.

'My God, Corin!'

Palfrey wasted no time and mustered all of his shamanistic healing power to see what he could do save Farnsworth's life. Yet given the state that the poor fellow was in, he was not confident of success.

It would have been an exceedingly strange sight to see this very English middle-aged lawyer, dressed as if to join a shooting party, kneeling by the side of the road in torrential rain, chanting weird incantations over what appeared to be a body, while making violent gestures as if he were suffering an epileptic attack.

As he looked down upon the dying Corin Farnsworth, Lionel noticed a small silver chain with a pendant attached to it lying on the ground. It was not dissimilar to the one from Chile that he wore around his own neck. However, this one was far more sinister and he immediately recognised that it was a bizarre facsimile of the figurine hanging from the buttress on the side of Thorpe Amberley church tower.

Palfrey began to understand exactly what he was dealing with.

* * *

DCI Williams had just arrived home after a long day. The sodding case on Dartmoor was beginning to get to him and all he really wanted to do was collect his pension and retire. He needed this fucking nutcase of a potential serial killer like a bucketful of horse manure for supper. Now there was some blasted Chief Super from Suffolk pulling rank and wanting to talk to him urgently, which would entail going back to the station, fishing out all his files, booting up the bloody computer and ...

'Your tea's ready dear.'

His wonderful missus had cooked his favourite: shepherd's pie. 'Forget it, love, I've gotta go back to the bloody nick. Shove it in the microwave, I'll get back as a soon as I can. What was it they said about a policeman's lot?' Williams cursed as he put his coat back on and slammed the door in disgust.

Chapter 20

Maggie Driscoll felt somewhat bereft. Donald, Jimmy, John and the guy with an American accent had all hurried off and, despite the babbling, well-meaning attention of Maisie and a couple of large glasses of scotch, she felt the need for some intelligent comfort in the wake of her ordeal. The normally feisty Drama teacher was badly shaken and could not remove the picture of the horrible grisly head from her mind. Sarah would not be much better than Maisie and, given her recent, highly-charged emotional state, could arguably be even worse. Maggie needed the support of somebody who was calm, collected and practical.

* * *

The heavy iron knocker rapped upon Charlotte's old wooden door.

She loved her small, old-fashioned, half-timbered cottage, which dated back some four hundred years and could probably tell quite a few tales. Maybe Roundheads or Cavaliers had lived in it; some day she would have to check. Although Massachusetts had its fair share of large old puritan farmhouses, there was very little to compare it with in the States, where everything always seemed to be bigger. Dusting around, she looked fondly upon the little wood burner that had been carefully set in the fireplace recess. It burned merrily in this chilly wet summer and would be so comforting when winter came. Her eyes glanced around at the exposed beams which exuded history, especially in flickering candlelight. She mused that it would be so romantic when she cooked Corin an American meal like one of her special New England dishes! Charlotte wondered where she could buy sufficiently large enough clams to make chowder and decided to ask Maggie for advice. She had just finished putting the finishing touches to clearing everything up by putting books, ornaments and furniture back into place. Corin had sorted out the major problems earlier. What a wonderful guy he was! Charlotte was still oozing the sensuality of their amazing lovemaking and she wondered, now, who the hell would be knocking at her door, with such vigour, at this time of the evening in what appeared to be an atrocious night outside.

It was with great surprise that she opened the door to see Maggie, whom she had just been thinking about, standing there, very bedraggled and soaking wet.

'N-ne-need a friend,' sobbed Maggie, who was obviously much shaken. 'And it's not what you might think, I haven't come to chat you up again.' She tried to raise a smile, then burst into floods of tears. Charlotte immediately gave her a consoling hug, gently steered her into the house, took her coat and sat her down on the old, comfy sofa.

'Here, honey, drink this.' Charlotte handed Maggie a large single malt and poured one for herself. 'Look, if it's about your partner trashing this place, forget …'

Maggie then explained the terrible shock she had experienced at the horrendous sight of the human head in the ground.

'Oh my God,' gasped Charlotte, 'how devastatingly awful.' She put her hand over her mouth in a reflex action, feeling sick.

Maggie was about to give further details of Donald Hetherington and the other men going to the scenes of the crimes when her own mobile rang. Lionel had her number for administrative reasons, to do with the dancing schedules, and so on, in respect of Maggie being the leader of the Tambourines. The Squire of the Tamberleys spoke in a grave voice and then revealed the horror that had befallen Corin Farnsworth. 'I tried everything I knew to save him,' said the troubled Palfrey. Maggie knew little of Lionel's dark, secret shamanistic powers which, on this occasion, had failed him.

Maybe his magic had been defeated by a higher force of the same.

'Look, I phoned you because I don't know Charlotte's number. Can you go and see her, she'll be devastated because Farnsworth and her appear to have rapidly become an item.'

'I'm already with her,' replied an even more distraught Maggie.

*　*　*

He was the ideal choice to provide a body to be occupied by a greater power that had monitored his every move and that of his Morris side. He was not a pleasant man and failed to notice the transformation that occurred when he was taken over. Living alone and leading a relatively dull life full of balance sheets and cash flow analysis, he knew that he should maybe have started his own accountancy business, but his security-obsessed elderly parents had forced him into the safer bet of working in the finance department of the local authority. He had spent countless weekdays sitting in a dingy office close to the Norman Tower near the Abbey Gardens of Bury St Edmunds. His highly efficient and now extinct little authority of West Suffolk was now amalgamated with its larger neighbour, East Suffolk, into the lumbering Suffolk County Council, administered from distant Ipswich. Initially, there was chaos and from that point onwards he lost any vestige of job satisfaction that he might have had.

Now that his parents were thankfully dead, he didn't socialise with any of his work colleagues, in the same way that he had little to do with the rest of the Tamberleys. He indulged in Morris Dancing as a kind of penance which helped him to maintain a level of fitness from the sedentary employment of sitting on his boring arse all day, and found a use managing the side's finances. He basically disliked everybody, which was the main reason why he was chosen by his Master in the first place. His main pastime was an obsession with criminology and he possessed a massive collection of non-fiction books and crime novels as well as videos and DVDs of both TV and cinema crime films.

He had followed the case of the Dartmoor burial murder on *Crimewatch* and had dribbled with pleasure over the gory description of the victim's death, especially noting the use of the spade. He would, however, have used something more drastic than chloroform to make the victims unconscious and suffer a bit more; something that would rapidly cause intense violent discomfort with severe flushing of the skin, impairment of vision and numbness of the extremities, together with delirium and dryness of the mouth, in the last horrible throes of death. His knowledge of the countryside was extensive, and this included the whereabouts of deadly nightshade plants in the vicinity of the Bury St Edmunds area. Belladonna poisoning would be his chosen method to achieve a painful departure from life. In a shed at the bottom of his garden, he had established a small rough-and-ready laboratory, using bits and pieces and test tubes from his schoolboys' chemistry set. It was cheaper, easier and less traceable to make one's own crude poison than to try and buy it from a pharmaceutical outlet. He read copies of the *British Medical Journal* and concluded, from various reports, that the effects of Belladonna were precisely the same whether it was administered through the skin or by mouth, and he made his plans accordingly.

The poisoner was meticulous in his preparation. He wore rubber surgical gloves and destroyed all containers and equipment save for the small phial he would need for the job. Somebody had to die to confuse the police between his murders and the other victims. This his Master had ordained in the grand plan. Noting the picture and design of the small silver pendant, vividly shown in the red-top tabloids reporting the Devon murder, he had cut it out carefully and pasted it into a special folder. The depressing little man with a massive chip on his shoulder particularly disliked those macho bastards in the Tamberleys like Farnsworth and Hetherington. Yet there was another, however, who possessed powers from another source that would always be a threat to his Master's mission. In due course, he would, indeed, need to be removed.

*   *   *

'Look, there's a pub, if that's what they call their fucking drinking houses in this godforsaken land.'

Rossini was extremely angry, and gagging for a drink. Christ knew what that sonofabitch McQuaid was doing apart from playing at fucking cops and robbers with the British FBI, or whatever they called their goddamned police. They had come out of the forest and just passed a sign indicating their arrival in Thorpe Amberley and, through the driving rain, had picked out the poorly lit sign of The Swan And Signet.

'Don't you just love these old-fashioned names?' Georgio mused. He was quietly enjoying his boss's burgeoning frustration and rage with all things British. 'Well at least you can grab a glass of whisky.'

'Oh, yeah, bet it won't be fucking bourbon!'

Georgio slewed the car next to the front door and they burst in, much to the surprise of the half-asleep Maisie.

Having ordered two large scotches on the rocks, Georgio enquired if the barmaid knew the whereabouts of the cottages of Charlotte and Corin Farnsworth. 'And we'll make it worth your while, honey.'

Despite extreme suspicion, the girl was not about to reject the large wad of what appeared to be dollar notes that he held out in his hand. This would be easy money and it would be simple to change it into sterling at any of the banks, or even cheaper at the nearby US Air Force base at Mildenhall, where she had connections.

'Sure,' she said, pouring them another couple of drinks and telling them exactly what they wanted to know by giving them precise directions.

* * *

After failing to save Corin's life, Lionel had wasted no time. Having pulled himself together from his mesmeric state, and with the sound of the *kultrun* still ringing in his head, the solicitor in him re-emerged and practicality took over. Clearly unable to leave a horribly murdered body by the side of the road, he phoned the police and then contacted Maggie Driscoll. The Martlesham HQ immediately notified DCS Thomas, already at the nearby scene of the two other crimes, that another victim called Farnsworth had been discovered.

'You must be joking,' Thomas screamed into the mouthpiece upon receiving the news. 'It's turning into a fucking massacre ... never had anything like this in all my years in the Force!' With fresh findings appearing by the minute, his mind was racing towards the reality of a skilled manpower problem. He would probably need to call in assistance, possibly from Scotland Yard. In the meantime he turned to Canadian who, very concerned, had crept up beside him.

'What exactly is your job in the Mounties?'

'Homicide,' replied McQaid who, apart from the location in a different country, was not totally lying, given his experience in the NYPD.

'Mind sticking around for a bit? I could certainly use your expertise and I'm sure we could work out some form of financial remuneration for your trouble.'

'Sure,' said Kelvin. 'I'm only here on vacation but it's always great for me to be doing any kind of detective work, especially a challenge like this little lot … and that's without any kind of payment.'

'Come on then.' Thomas shook him by the hand. 'Good to have such a friend on board!'

McQuaid realised that he was getting in too deep now and that, sooner or later, he would need to come clean to this very senior British officer and tell him the whole truth, especially if Rossini and the highly intellectual thug, Georgio, had anything to do with the killing of Farnsworth. Thomas was no fool and would soon see through his Canadian guise and realise that he had not even shown him his warrant card; besides which, McQuaid was beginning to both like and respect him. This unexpected, albeit grisly, opportunity might lead to the prospect of a totally new future. Kelvin rather fancied becoming a British cop.

In the fast-moving situation, none of them noticed the journalist surreptitiously lurking within earshot. He followed them, keeping a well-practised, safe distance, but missing nothing.

*   *   *

Within half an hour of Palfrey's call, a high-speed squad car screeched to a halt on the forest road. The journalist's car was parked, a short distance away, hidden by trees. Thomas, McQuaid and the enthusiastic young Perkins jumped out.

'You Palfrey?' DCS Thomas dispensed with niceties. He was facing the biggest challenge of his career. It was becoming a nightmare, and all before the TV and tabloids got wind of it. At this point, he knew that he could kiss goodbye to a decent night's sleep or anything that remotely resembled his normal family life. 'God help my missus and the kids,' he said to himself.

With its blue light flashing and siren screaming, the ambulance roared in and the green-suited paramedics took control. The group leader kneeled over the body and then bent his head closer. He felt what he had suspected: there was a slight pulse.

'D'you realise he's still alive?'

Palfrey raised and closed his eyes as the sound of the *kultran* grew louder.

Thomas was already on the phone. 'Forget your ambulance, we can use the police chopper, it's on its way. Pray that we can make this one corpse less!'

He called Perkins over. 'You're coming along too, and McQuaid!' As the helicopter took off, the journalist followed in his car, guessing its destination.

Chapter 21

The gurney rattled down the endlessly long corridors of the West Suffolk Hospital towards the Intensive Care Unit, with the accompanying emergency medical team in full chase. Their white coats flapped as it rapidly lurched around corners with a hurriedly arranged drip swinging precariously to and fro. They had already given the patient yet another cardiac massage and the body was just hanging on to life.

'I'm not fit as I used to be for this!' Thomas huffed and puffed as he struggled to keep up with the athletic young doctors and nurses.

'Know what you mean,' added McQuaid, also panting, wishing he had quit smoking.

In the chopper, Kelvin had decided to open up to Thomas. He told him the whole truth that he was an ex-NYPD Detective with the rank of Captain, now a top New York private detective, currently employed by Mafia-connected Carl Rossini, hired to track down his wife, Charlotte. McQuaid told Thomas of his suspicion that Rossini and his hit-man, Georgio, could well be responsible for the attempted murder of the guy they might just have saved. He also expressed his great fear that the two of them could now be planning to execute Charlotte.

'I was forced to give him directions of where they both lived, and deeply regret it. I really need to get to Charlotte to both warn and protect her, otherwise you might have another body on your hands.'

Palfrey had announced that he was going to see Charlotte

113

to explain the latest development. 'I understand that Corin has no real family and she has recently become closely involved with him in a bit of a whirlwind romance,' he had said to Thomas. As the chopper lifted into the air, McQuaid had caught a glimpse of Palfrey climbing into his Land Rover.

'Look, I'm not needed here,' the American explained. 'Both Charlotte and this Palfrey guy are in great danger. You have no idea how lethal Rossini and his henchman can be. Georgio is a highly intelligent ex-Green beret and trained to kill, with a lot of pain if necessary. I'm going over to Charlotte's cottage. At least I might prevent another double murder. Palfrey will be like a lamb to the slaughter in Georgio's hands.'

'OK, but take my chap with you.' Thomas barked an order. 'Andy, go with Mr McQuaid and take this.' He handed Perkins an unofficial pistol that, if ever it was discovered, would cost him his job. Yet he always carried it for personal protection. No fucking crook was going to take his life, and no job was worth it. 'Use it to protect yourself if you have to, we're dealing with dangerous Mafia killers here and there's no time to call in the firearms team. I'll take full responsibility for anything that might happen. This is a dangerous state of affairs and calls for drastic measures.' Perkins nodded but resolved to give the 'piece' to McQuaid. After all, an ex-NYPD bloke would be used to playing cops and robbers.

* * *

Like a limpet, the reporter discreetly followed the police car in his beat-up yellow Escort that had seemingly never been cleaned. Gerald Hobson was freelance and highly money motivated to sell to the highest bidder. Although his bread and butter work was for the local East Anglian papers, he was also something of a lineage man for national press, media, radio and television. He knew he was on to something very big and had already phoned the genesis of the story to Radio Orwell, the local station at Ipswich. The basics of the latest development, mentioning Farnsworth by name and saying he had been rushed to the West Suffolk Hospital, had already been given on the hourly bulletin.

* * *

Georgio half crawled through the undergrowth at the back of the cottage. His expensive Armani suit was already soaked by the torrential rain, so the sopping wet grass, nettles and bushes would not make any difference. It could be dry cleaned later. He would, however, have preferred to have been clad in the camouflage combats he had worn on his 'ops' in various jungle campaigns. 'Shit,' he cursed as a noxious bramble tore open a sleeve. 'Forget dry cleaning now,' he muttered.

He peered through the lattice window and saw that the wood burner with the door partly open still burned in what must be the lounge of Charlotte's cottage. A lopsided mesh fire-screen looked as if it had been hastily placed in front of it and was an indication that maybe the owner had left in a hurry. The hitman thought that he had ascertained this when peering through the windows at the front. Georgio was not entirely happy about the situation and not because the boss was sitting nice and warm back in the Aston Martin, slowly retracting down from an outburst of rage, smoking a Havana, sipping Jack Daniels and twiddling the radio to find some classical music to calm himself down. 'If she's there, waste her,' Rossini had just said, still furious that they had found Farnsworth's cottage empty and was even more determined to execute his wife.

Hard bastard that he was, it was not in the Italian's normal mandate to shoot down a beautiful woman in cold blood. He had always liked Charlotte and had sometimes taken her on shopping expeditions. She had accepted his homosexuality and shown some sympathy for gay rights which is more than could be said for many high-class women in New York society. To the boss, his sexuality did not matter. In fact Carl had happily trusted the care of his spouse to his right-hand man, knowing that she would be safe from his paws. However, if he had been straight, Georgio could well imagine his temptation to give her one on the side without Rossini ever finding out. Now, as he miserably dragged himself through the overgrown garden, he was required to shoot her. Yet, the big man paid him handsomely, which afforded him his luxurious house, cars, expensive holidays and all the trappings of a millionaire lifestyle. He had to forget personal feelings as he had been trained to do by the military, many years before. Charlotte was just another piece of meat to be disposed of.

He worked his way to the back door and, never known for subtlety, gave it a mighty kick which almost broke the hinges. He rapidly moved through the house, clutching his light machine-gun in the firing position, going systematically upstairs from bathroom to bedroom and back down again through the kitchen, dining room and even the two toilets. Upstairs, he turned over the bed before returning down again to heave the sofa upside down and sweep through every corner of the lounge. In sheer frustration at the absence of the occupant, and feeling wet and miserable, he let loose a hail of bullets into one of the lounge chairs. 'Carl is going to go fucking ballistic,' he muttered. By the time he had finished the cottage looked as if a battle had taken place.

Outside in the car, Rossini heard the gunfire, even above the crescendo of Nessun Dorma, and smiled with the satisfaction of revenge. He drew heavily on his cigar. It was the lull before the storm. Bored with Pavarotti, Carl continued to rotate the radio tuning knob and froze as he heard the bulletin. The news would be Georgio's saving grace for not finding Charlotte. When he emerged, Rossini pre-empted his apologies. 'The bitch isn't in there is she? Get this heap to the West Suffolk Hospital. Farnsworth's there, apparently dying, and that's where my wife will be, so just who the hell has tried to kill him before us? And by the way, who were you blasting to hell in there, or was it just practice?'

*   *   *

Maggie opened the door. She had not always seen eye to eye with Lionel and regarded him as a boring old fuddy-duddy. Reciprocally, he had always resented her belligerent attitude, yet the two of them had some respect for each other in trying to hold together their respective teams of dancers who, in so many ways, were mutually dependent.

Tonight, Maggie was pleased to see him. Somehow, the sight of the man beneath the deerstalker, looking every bit the country squire and normally at variance with her hippyish world, represented solidity and reassurance. She had obviously been crying and now Palfrey put his comforting arms around her as she sobbed. 'There, there,' he whispered.

'Charlotte's in there in a hell of state ... I've had to tell her ... she has totally fallen in love with Corin ... in such a short space of time.' Maggie led Lionel through to the lounge where the wood burner still glowed merrily. He thought, momentarily, that his own logs at home had probably burned through by now.

Charlotte rose and the two women clung to Palfrey who had not had such close touchy-feely with womankind since the days of his ill-fated marriage. 'Look,' he said, 'Corin is still just alive. The paramedics have taken him to the West Suffolk Hospital. No time to waste, the Land Rover's outside, let's go.'

Donning coats in great haste, Charlotte put the guard in front of the wood burner, the door of which was partly open. The old short wheelbase vehicle chugged off from the cottage into the stormy night with Maggie opting to sit uncomfortably, being thrown about, on the rough metallic bench seat in the back.

Within half an hour, the Aston Martin drew up in the lane outside.

* * *

With the absence of the horrible Newmans, Simon Carew's life at the farm was now wonderful. He had the place to himself without the human beings that he hated, which included that snobby lot of Morris bastards. Now all he had to worry about were his beloved animals; they were much better than people and he took great delight in encouraging the previously neglected farm dogs and cats into sleeping in the Newmans' beds. He cackled at the sight of this. At the back of his mind, however, was the thought that sooner or later Jake and Jamie Newman would be missed but, for now, he was happy. In due course men in blue uniforms might come to the farm but he would be nice to them and make a pot of tea. Carew lit himself a crude cannabis joint and contemplated his options, contented in his own little bubble.

* * *

'Look, he's only just hanging on to life.'

The grim faced young Registrar tried to be sympathetic but knew it would only be a matter of time. 'The blow to the head was nasty but I don't think it's the main problem. He's a tough guy but there's something else. We won't know about it until … I hate to say this, after his death, which I fear is imminent. An autopsy, of course, should then tell us the truth. Sister!'

Upon hearing these words, Charlotte burst into uncontrollable sobbing, as both Maggie and Lionel put their comforting arms around her.

Sister Jordan spoke kindly. 'Normally we would allow no visitors but, under the circumstances, you can all go in and sit beside him, especially as I gather there's no family.'

Before they went in, DCS Thomas stepped forward.

'Mrs Rossini, Mr Palfrey and … ?'

'Maggie Driscoll.'

Thomas held his hand out to Palfrey. 'So relieved you're all here.' He turned to Charlotte. 'Mrs Rossini, you're in great danger and I've sent my men out to your cottage.' The Chief Superintendent briefly explained.

'Oh my God!' gasped Charlotte. 'My bastard husband, I should have known. So he's behind all of this!' She clasped her hand to her mouth and staggered a little as Maggie gave a supporting arm.

'Look, you're safe here and I've sent for reinforcements in case he shows up. My other men, including, incidentally, one of your fellow Americans, will also return once they discover you're not at your cottage. Do as Sister says, there may not be much time, go in and see Corin before …' He stopped without saying the dreaded words.

Charlotte started to sob again as they left the anteroom and entered the small, very spartan, clinically scrubbed side ward. Corin was fixed up to drips and wired to a cardiac monitor which recorded and displayed his heartbeat. On the small circular screen, a tiny green dot barely bobbed up and down to indicate that the heart was just beating; maybe its last throes of life.

As they sat beside the bed, tragically knowing it was just a matter of time, Lionel heard the sound of the *kultrun* drum beginning to ring in his head once again.

*   *   *

McQuaid and Perkins reached Charlotte's cottage and it soon became apparent that they had been beaten to it. Kelvin's experience showed through as he instinctively took charge, to the relief of Perkins. 'Somebody's kicked the shit out of this place,' he moaned, looking around the devastation that Georgio had created in such a lovely old cottage and, drawing Thomas's pistol, snapped. 'I have a sure idea who did this.'

'Should we head back to the hospital?' Perkins had a gut feeling that, as things were moving so fast, the danger, itself, was returning to Bury.

'Yep, drive like hell!' the American answered. He could not be totally certain but he seemed to be hearing the strange pounding of a drum in his head.

Chapter 22

FROM THE MEMOIRS OF DR. LIONEL PALFREY, PhD, BA (Hons) LLB

It is not easy to describe the strange cocktail of events and highly charged emotions which occurred at the West Suffolk Hospital on that terrible afternoon. Even as I write this, some two months later, my hand still shakes from the sheer enormity, tension, horror and drama of what, it is difficult to believe, actually took place.

*The throbbing of the **kultrun** in my head increased in intensity and that told me that awful things were about to happen. I could feel the power of the Machi transcending through the cosmos and across enormous distances.*

The tiny dot stopping its bounce on the screen of the cardiac monitor was the first dramatic thing to happen.

Then we all became aware of a lot of commotion and the slamming of doors, shouts and cries of alarm disturbing the more usual sounds of the hospital.

Next came sirens and screeching of brakes and a burst of gunfire. Some hospital staff were apparently wounded. These terrifying sounds rapidly spread nearer, echoing down the long corridors towards our secluded unit. Although DCS Thomas had his men strategically placed, they were no match for the two Mafia men, especially the one who, it later transpired, was capable of taking on the best of our own SAS. The Detective Chief Superintendent had remained within the Intensive Care Unit (ICU) itself.

I felt my skin stiffen and take on a new dimension even more powerful than that which had occurred by the roadside as I had bent over poor Farnsworth. The pounding of the drum became almost unbearable as my whole body began to assume shapes that were completely new to me. Although I cannot recollect a direct speaking voice, there was, nevertheless, a dynamic force which was controlling actions that were not wholly mine. Yet I seem to recollect that the knowledge imparted to me by the Machi all those years ago was being activated into movements designed to create a killer, maybe to save further butchery.

What exactly took place next still takes some time to put into any logical order, for I was possessed by another power over which I was not in full control and the sequence of events is somewhat hazy in the manner, I suppose, of being on some drug-induced trip. And everything happened so fast. However, the momentous arrival of two men shouting obscenities remains vivid; I also recall my eyes rolling wildly as I flung my arms about much in the manner of that previously experienced when bending over Farnsworth. Yet my actions now were much more dramatic. It instantly shook the two women out of their sobbing grief at the realisation that Corin was dead, especially as the seemingly demented Rossini began to shout.

'You're fucking dead, bitch!' he yelled, pushing Georgio aside in his maniacal zest to murder his wife. He raised what appeared to be a light machine-gun to shoot the crying Charlotte down, as Maggie, Sister Jordan and DCS Thomas cowered below the dead Farnsworth's bed.

It was at this point that my actions must have peaked for Georgio, who we discovered later had really wanted no part of this, had become transfixed by me and had laid his weapon down. Similarly, as Charlotte, the other two women and Thomas later told me, Rossini was drawn to my rolling eyes and mesmerised by my strange chanting, incantations and wild movements to the extent of being momentarily distracted for a vital few seconds.

The brief moment was all that was necessary for McQuaid to burst through from another side door and shoot Rossini dead to the ground with Thomas's old pistol. Within seconds, Perkins and the Police Armed Response Team crashed in. They had not been needed.

Georgio raised his hands in the air, presumably wondering how he might try to argue his way out of it all. The DCS stepped forward to arrest him.

*Upon reflection, I think I am beginning to understand how the strange forces of the Machi work, whereby, as well as the prevention of killing, the curative side of the **kultrun**'s powers can effect direct killing where necessary to stop even more bloodshed. McQuaid subsequently informed me that, as he raced through the hospital, he experienced the inexplicable sound of a beating drum which reached a crescendo as he raised the pistol, and seemed to tell him to shoot Rossini.*

The question still remains (so DCS Thomas tells me) as to who killed Corin Farnsworth as well the other two bodies found near Thorpe Amberley.

'It's three murders now,' Thomas sighed. 'At least you and McQuaid have prevented a fourth.' He put a comforting arm around Charlotte. 'You're safe now, madam, thanks to the combined efforts of Dr Palfrey and our other American friend here. Incidentally, just what the hell were you doing Palfrey?'

'Don't even ask me to begin to explain,' I had replied.

* * *

The bodies had been transferred to the Forensic Medicine Lab at the Martlesham Police HQ where they lay on three separate slabs. Because of the magnitude of the situation, Thomas wanted the post-mortems carried out as quickly as possible, especially as the cases had now attracted major media coverage. Various versions of the killings were the number one item on all radio and television news programmes and were front-page headlines in the national press, notably the tabloids, where wildly speculative stories and theories abounded. Because Thomas wanted everything kept under wraps until more substantial evidence was available, the press began to invent. They were especially fervent in their insatiable curiosity about the barely leaked details of Dr Palfrey's part. There was nothing more sure to make the media paranoid than any hint of 'cover up', and this resulted in such cheap headlines as the 'Rustigate Murders' and 'Gunfight at the OK ICU'. Moreover, the DCS had the Chief Constable breathing down his neck, furious that such a serial killing catastrophe should have happened on his hitherto relatively tranquil patch. 'Murders like this are for fucking cities!' he had screamed down the phone, under pressure, himself, from as high up as the Home Secretary, who had been required to answer questions in the House. Therefore, each autopsy was carried out in the utmost secrecy and began with the gruesome opening up of Farnsworth's corpse.

* * *

'Well, I tell you,' Dr Shirley Reynolds announced to her forensic team. 'It wasn't the blow to the head that killed this poor guy. Look at the traces of this stuff, it's bloody crude, but lethal.' The other doctors took away the samples and rapidly concluded, after tests, that it was belladonna poison, probably home produced, that had finally stopped the heart of Corin Farnsworth.

'And you say that this is not present in the bodies of the two Newmans?'

'No, Chief Super,' replied Doctor Reynolds.

'In which case, we're probably looking at more than one killer. Welcome to sleepy old Suffolk … bollocks!'

'Language, sir!' Shirley Reynolds protested, shaking her head with a reproachful smile.

Chapter 23

They had come outside where it was possible to smoke and the four of them stood by the main entrance doors to the hospital, shattered and mesmerised. They clutched small cardboard cups of lukewarm vending machine coffee. As Maggie began to roll up, Palfrey lit his pipe. McQuaid took out his packet of Winstons.

'Light me one, please.' Still shaking, Charlotte spoke to Kelvin for the first time. 'You saved my life back there and, despite our common accent, I don't even know you … although I've heard you're from Toronto, yet I don't think it's a Canadian accent.'

McQuaid gave his fellow American the cigarette. 'There's a lot explain, but I couldn't have done it without this guy.' He gestured towards Palfrey.

'Didn't know you smoked,' said Maggie. 'You could've had one of these.'

'And choke to death on shit!' Charlotte's comment broke the tension and they all chuckled with the realisation that they had come through a brief but terrifying ordeal, and, more significantly, were still alive.

'Not sure about Maggie's tobacco, but this coffee is crap,' McQuaid declared, saying that, in the States, it wouldn't even be used to wash out the trash chute.

'So, it's true that you're American?'

'You bet, Charlotte, truly of the Big Apple! How's about I take you out for a drink and you'll find out all there is to know about Kelvin McQuaid Junior.'

'Sure!' the beauty answered with some hesitation in her voice.

Lionel looked on with a slight pang as he could see, once again, that any chances his heroism might achieve would likely be thwarted by the younger man, a fellow Yank and, more precisely, a New Yorker.

* * *

By now, the media reportage was at fever pitch. Gerald Hobson had thrown a metaphorical snowball that had rolled into an avalanche. It would ultimately accelerate his career towards a top news presenter's job within the satellite TV network.

The early evening broadcast fervour on all channels was in meltdown as it was the biggest multiple killing sensation for years, since the days of Hindley and Brady or the infamous Fred and Rose West. Because of the complexities of so many unanswered questions and the leaked speculation about more than one killer for the three bodies, notwithstanding the press delight about the 'Hospital Shootout', the early evening news on all television channels and radio broadcasts was almost entirely devoted to the new sensation. Special interest was centred upon the strange actions of Lionel Palfrey, already dubbed 'Dr Death' by the red-top tabloids, with wildly inaccurate conjecture about dark forces, as well as building up the 'John Wayne' image of McQuaid as the hero of the hour. In Winchester, Massachusetts, Charlotte's parents watched the same bulletins that had been relayed worldwide, especially to the States because of the American interest.

* * *

Simon Carew sat in his dingy room in the annexe to the main farmhouse. He watched the six o'clock news on the little portable TV that the Newmans had grudgingly loaned him. He was perplexed as to who else might have spoiled his party.

*   *   *

Williams climbed down from the train at Bury St Edmunds station and surveyed the depressing back streets that bore no resemblance to the delights of the historic town beyond. The Suffolk Police 'jam sandwich' squad car waited to take him to the incident centre of portakabins that had been set up on the outskirts of Thorpe Amberley, now a community under siege. Apart from the blue and white plastic tape demarcation lines of the cordoned-off scenes of crime, there was an encampment of trailers and camper vans indicating that the newsmen intended to stay for the long haul. The sleepy village, with the eyes of the world upon it, would never be the quite same again.

The two detectives who were about to meet were very, very different men. Williams was from the University of Life, a sometimes truculent, 'old school' copper who could be occasionally insubordinate and outspoken to senior officers and who did not suffer fools easily, even if they were his superiors. With his track record, however, he was generally regarded as being the best DI in the West Country. The Met had tried to poach him once and he had told them to piss off. Conversely, Thomas had graduated from King's College, London, with First Class Honours in History and Criminology. He had always been the 'blue-eyed boy' and a rising star who had distinguished himself by being willing to try out new methods, especially if they provided the chance for relatively inexperienced policemen to advance their careers. Thomas was heavily into the concept of 'staff development', and was hence the kind of policeman Williams and his ilk would sneeringly dub a 'pen-pushing paper cop'.

'Willy' Williams held out his hand.. 'Well, with a name like

Thomas you might be a Welshman. That's a good start!' He laughed. The Chief Super, under tremendous strain and suffering from lack of sleep, was not impressed.

'Let's cut the crap, Williams. Good of you to come, but with our Chief Constable, Home Secretary and half the world's fucking reporters on my back I haven't time for much humour. Now tell me all you know about this psycho who buried some poor bastard alive on your patch. We appear to have two copycat cases here with an added complication of another possible murderous fruitcake, as well as two Mafia nutters who came looking for yet another victim who was already dead and who tried to kill the poor wife of one of them. We shot one and have the other in custody. All very complicated, isn't life a ball!'

'Okay.' Much chastened, Williams straightened himself up. He had clocked the enormity of the problem and felt sorry for this younger, yet very senior copper. He would now give Thomas all the benefit of his many years of experience to justify his long, tedious journey from the other side of the country. 'I'm all yours Chief Superintendent. To begin with we've identified our body as Andrew Carew.'

*   *   *

'It's good to have a fellow American around, especially a New Yorker.' A still tearful Charlotte grasped McQuaid's hands across the table in the far corner of The Swan. 'Gee, I've never been in this pub before.' She spoke in jerky sentences. 'I never thought you were Canadian from the moment I heard your accent.'

'One hundred percent Brooklyn, honey, although most of my family were from the Bronx.'

'Streetwise then.' Charlotte forced a smile and inhaled on a cigarette. 'I'd given these up, but with everything that's happened. Oh, Kelvin, if ...' The tears rolled.

'Shush, sweetheart!' McQuaid tenderly gripped her hands. 'I'm going to tell you everything.'

*   *   *

Thomas gathered the whole team together in Thorpe Amberley Village Hall to introduce DI Williams and complimented his many years of expertise in homicide. Because of his involvement, and being the local boy, Donald Hetherington had been temporarily relieved of uniform duties in Ipswich and seconded to the Thorpe Amberley cases. He sat quietly at the back, dressed casually and glad to be out of uniform. Maybe this could be the start of a new career move to CID ...

Williams addressed the meeting and spoke about the similarities between the body found on Dartmoor and the two bodies discovered at Thorpe. 'One of the most significant common factors is the killer's calling card in the form of a little silver pendant of a bizarre figurine.' The DI showed a photograph projected, hugely, on to a screen behind as McQuaid slipped in quietly and sat beside Hetherington.

'Excuse me interrupting, sir ...'

All eyes turned upon the voice. Donald Hetherington looked closely at the large picture and noticed something that he had not realised before when he had first seen the small pendant in the driving rain, by the head of the body of Jamie Newman, in the darkness of that foul night.

'The pendant, it's of a gargoyle-type figure identical to the one that people find very scary on the side of the church tower buttress, here in Thorpe Amberley. Some say it is an effigy of the devil himself.'

Thomas, slightly irritated, interjected. 'Yes, thank you PC Hetherington, not sure what superstition has to do with a murder inquiry. Please continue Williams.' Yet, as the words of slight reprimand left his mouth, he privately pondered on it, in the light of what he had witnessed with Palfrey at the hospital. Hetherington's words also struck a chord with Williams who decided to make a phone call to Devon when he had finished giving his address.

'And there is another factor,' added the Devonshire detective. 'We found this near to our body.' He showed another photograph of the blown up butt that appeared to be from a roll-up cigarette. This time another voice spoke.

'Another common factor indeed,' interrupted Andy Perkins. 'We also found what appeared to be a cigarette butt of sorts by the body of our first victim, Jake Newman.' To Thomas's intense annoyance, some wag near the back muttered, 'I doubt if he smoked it.' There was an audible titter, a bit of light relief, amongst the stressed-out coppers in the room. 'I heard that,' he thundered. 'Can we stay focused!'

A WPC chipped in. 'I had the job of taking it to Forensics and they produced their conclusion just before this meeting. I was going to tell the Chief Super, but there wasn't time as the meeting had begun.'

'Well?' Thomas roared again.

'Their tests discovered that the cigarette butt was in fact the remains of a marihuana joint.'

'My God, our lab boys were thinking of reaching the same conclusion, but our specimen wasn't so good having endured the hostile Dartmoor weather for a considerable period of time,' exclaimed Williams. 'I'll get it sent up here pronto!'

A broad smile appeared across Thomas's face, revealing some relief at what might be a significant breakthrough. 'Marvellous,' he beamed. 'If we can now find a suspect, then it might be possible to link DNA from these butts to the killer – all we need now is the live body of a murderer!'

'It would be great if we could solve our case as well,' said

Williams. 'I feel that we're one stage nearer to cracking the unsolved mystery of who sadistically buried poor bloody Andrew Carew alive.'

Donald Hetherington shot bolt upright in his chair at the mention of the name Carew.

He stood up. 'Maybe we're on to something even bigger, here,' he announced.

*　*　*

A car sat outside Lionel Palfrey's house. Its occupant sat patiently waiting to pounce. Gerald Hobson would systematically do the same outside the cottages of Maggie and Charlotte. He had the kernel of a scoop and, in his verminous way, would not rest until he had sensationalised every detail for the tabloids and their bloodthirsty readers.

Chapter 24

Thomas questioned Hetherington in his mobile office. 'And you say he hasn't been seen around for a few days? The name could just be coincidence, but from what I've gathered ... yes I do my homework ... there was no love lost between the two of you in this Morris side of yours. Sure it isn't a grudge suspicion? We need clearer evidence to bring him in. Anyway, it doesn't fit with the attempted murder of Farnsworth. No marihuana butt there.'

'There was another pendant found there, though, sir.'

'Yes, but it was the belladonna that finally killed Corin. So we probably can't pin that on Carew. And what about our two Americans who burst into the hospital? Maybe they had something to do with the poisoning. Whatever the situation, the home-made belladonna ingredient poses a whole new set of complications in a much bigger picture.'

'I'm not a detective, sir, but I do know the local patch. Can I dig around to try and find a link to Carew?'

Thomas thought carefully before replying. 'Okay, it's worth a bloody good go.'

'Can I get Kelvin McQuaid to help me? The two of us get on great and seem to work well together.'

'Why not?' Thomas replied. 'I'd like to give the two of you a chance here if you think you can do it. Nothing like local knowledge, and McQuaid, with his NYPD expertise, is straining at the leash. You're a promising young copper and can learn a lot from his American methods. I'm all for giving new people with fresh approaches a try, especially if we can use them to bring these cases to a close and cock a snook at the ever-critical press. There's nothing like being thrown in the deep end combined with ambitious enthusiasm and, in this case, McQuaid's vast experience. Who knows what the future might hold for both of you? Myself, Williams and the rest of the team will continue to look at all the loose ends of these interrelated, complex cases. We'll keep it all under wraps for now. I have enough on my plate dealing with the media, especially that nosy, irritating bastard Gerald Hobson. You two can concentrate purely on Carew. If he's our man he's probably a clever sod – give him enough rope and he might hang himself, but get that irrefutable proof!'

'Thank you sir, I'll do my very best.'

* * *

Lionel Palfrey was somewhat distressed and puzzled, which had not been helped by being badgered by that wretched journalist. Because of his intimate involvement, Thomas had shown him the courtesy of informing him that it was a crude form of belladonna poisoning that had actually killed Corin Farnsworth. 'And whatever kind of unexplained mumbo-jumbo it is that you're into, it's doubtful if it could counteract the effects of the infamous "deadly nightshade".' The good magic of the Machi had warned him and had worked to its limits travelling, so far, across the vast spaces of time and distance, yet he had a gut feeling that there was a greater, more ancient '*wekufe*' evil over which even the power of the *kultrun* could not hold sway. And because of this he was both confused and frustrated.

* * *

McQuaid had jumped at the chance. 'Can we keep you in it a bit longer?' Thomas had said, expressing his deep gratitude for what the American had already contributed, especially the killing of Rossini, preventing the murder of Charlotte.

'I have an idea,' Donald Hetherington told Kelvin. 'Great to still have you on board, let's visit your watering hole.'

'Ashtrays?' queried Jimmy Tusser, still in a state of aftershock in the wake of experiencing the gruesomeness of death. The publican, postman and part-time poacher was used to picking up the sometimes shotgun-mutilated bodies of hares, rabbits and pheasants, but hideous, murdered corpses were a different matter. 'Well, when Maisie ever gets around to emptying them, they're chucked into an old plastic bucket kept under the bar, and this, eventually, is tipped into the wheelie bin in the yard. Yes, of course you can look in it, bloody mucky, though!'

After putting on surgical gloves, McQuaid and Hetherington took the disgusting container outside and tipped the contents on to a plastic sheet that Jimmy managed to find. With some tweezers they began the arduous, smelly task of separating the cork filter 'dog ends', some lipstick stained, from the stubs of roll-up cigarettes, of which the latter predominated.

'We get builder's labourers and farm workers in here,' Tusser explained. 'They enjoy their games of darts and dominoes after a hard day's graft. I don't mind 'em coming in with their muddy boots, unlike The Cat where they're barred. Yes, Simon Carew's one of them, but he never joins in, just sits staring at the optics and his bloody wellies stink of cow-shit sometimes. But he spends a lot of money on pints of lager.'

Ultimately, the two men had created a significant pile of discarded roll-ups which they sent to the forensic lab at Ipswich.

*　*　*

He hoped that nobody would see him, especially with police crawling all around the village. This fact alone gave him such a high adrenaline rush it could probably not be surpassed, even by the hard drugs that he had experimented with, just the once. Incorporated into it was a force so powerful that it sent the equivalent of a burning electrical charge pulsating through every nerve and sinew of his body. He was doing his Master's work. It was his usual time of three o'clock in the morning. In another hour the summer dawn chorus would begin its routine assault upon Suffolk eardrums to herald the start of the new day. Many would curse this pre-alarm call and roll over for another bout of sleep. Yet the dedicated early risers, farmers and postmen, would regard it as a thing of beauty, especially where it was at its loudest in the deep countryside. He did not like beauty, in fact he loathed it. His world was a dark place and he would be its servant to this end. There was a need to be quick, for soon after the ritual of the wretched birds, wretched people would start to be about. He knelt before the figurine.

'I have succeeded, so far, Master. There are a few deaths. Your other servants have operated, so far, yet the fool one will be caught and the other, because of powers from afar, has been shot dead. These Morris Dancers, especially, must be taught not to mock things they so little understand. There is the further one, sheltering amongst them, who has powers that challenge you. Enter my body, again ... oh Master ... and he will be eliminated.'

The man reached up on tiptoe, barely managing to kiss the feet of the figurine before departing the churchyard in great haste.

* * *

McQuaid told Charlotte everything and spared no details about himself, how his world had fallen apart and how

136

Rossini had offered him a financial lifeline but one which he began to hate himself for.

'And now it looks as if I'm a British cop, at least a temporary one.' He laughed. 'Co-opted, anyway, to track down the main murderer, working alongside Donald Hetherington – what a combination!'

'After what you did to save me, I'm sure the Brits could not have placed their trust in a better man.'

'Yeah, but even if we do nail the main bastard, there's an added complication of another murderer who may have been responsible for the death of your Corin.'

Charlotte began to cry. 'It's just that we'd only known each other for a very short time but it was fantastic love and passion from the word go ...' McQuaid put his arm around her and gave her a gentle squeeze.

'There, there!' he whispered, 'have a bloody cry but don't upset yourself too much ... nothing will beat us Yanks, eh?'

She smiled and gave him a little kiss on the cheek. He could feel himself going to jelly.

* * *

'Bingo!' Dr Reynolds let out a little shriek of delight. 'Who said fiddling about with filthy bits of bodies and the materials they use was boring? The saliva samples from the marihuana butt next to Jake Newman's body and the similar stub from Devon all have the same DNA, and most of the roll-up fag butts from the pub ashtray are also the same. However, I doubt if the latter can be used in evidence as they were not taken from the scene of a crime. Yet we have a bloody match!'

'Didn't think you approved of swearing.' Thomas gave her a friendly shoulder hug. 'Good girl, now we're in business!'

Chapter 25

Thomas and Williams sat together in that exulted state of anticipation. Hetherington and McQuaid occupied the back seat of the car.

'You two were in at the beginning,' Thomas had said kindly. 'You might as well be in at the kill.' He had invited them to come along for the arrest, partly because he felt bad that all of their messy efforts with the revolting cigarette butts would not be admissible in court, although they did reinforce Carew's guilt.

They were in the unmarked car which drove at the front of the small convoy. Discreetly, behind them followed the two police cars and a van in which sat the armed response team. The cavalry was parked behind a thick hawthorn hedge some way down the rough gravel track that wound up to the Newman's farm. Thomas was taking no chances. Their target was clearly a dangerous serial killer and all they needed to do was arrest him on suspicion and take the vital mouth swabs for DNA evidence to match the marihuana butts and prove his guilt.

* * *

Carew heard them coming; he had been strumming his guitar and humming a Morris tune.

'Maybe I won't m-make them a cup of tea!' he muttered to himself as he put down the guitar and picked up a double-barrelled twelve-bore shotgun. Calmly, he stuffed a cartridge into each firing chamber as he peered through the net curtain and observed the plain Rover car outside with what appeared to be men in suits sitting in it.

'They m-m-might have honoured me with a s-s-squad car,' he continued to stutter as he cocked both barrels of the gun, took off the safety catch and assessed that the vehicle was probably within the prescribed seventy-yard range of the cheap, catalogue purchased Russian hunting weapon.

*   *   *

As Thomas opened the car door a deafening report split the air and the vehicle was peppered with lethal pellets which shattered the windscreen. The DCS let out a scream of pain as blood began to drip from his arm. 'Get down!' he yelled. 'The bastard's shot me!'

Heatherington said urgently, 'I know this loony, sir, let me see if I can crawl round the back of the place ... look, I can get into the undergrowth quickly from the back here, while he's still feeling pleased with himself and before he shoots again.'

'Okay Hetherington.' Thomas was in no mood to dilly-dally with blood now pouring from him, as Williams scrabbled around for handkerchiefs to use as a makeshift tourniquet and bandage, racking his brains for his first-aid knowledge. McQuaid peered into the glove compartment and, as he had guessed, there was a medical kit inside.

'Have you still got that gun Kelvin?' Hetherington asked McQuaid. 'Doesn't matter whether it's loaded or not.' The American pulled it out of his jacket pocket and handed it over.

Using all of his combined police training, Boy Scout memories and general country knowledge acquired as a boy, Donald slithered through the dense mixture of stinging nettles and rose bay willow herb with the brambles tearing at his sleeves. He was oblivious to being cut to ribbons and stung all over – he was on a mission to nail the screwed up little runt who had been a thorn in his flesh since the day he had joined the Tamberleys. 'And the little fucker is a sadistic serial killer,' he kept telling himself as he finally worked his way to the back of Carew's abode. With a pounding heart, he approached the back door. Thank God it wasn't locked and he was able to slide into the kitchen. It was a tiny place and he could just glimpse Carew sitting in the front room. The bastard was in the process of raising the gun to his shoulder and Donald had to act quickly. Afterwards, he remembered hurling himself forward and clouting Simon gently across the back of the head with the handle of the pistol. It was a gamble as Carew swung round and pulled the shotgun trigger. Thankfully, he was dazed from the soft blow and the loud blast passed to Donald's right. Hetherington wrenched the weapon out of Carew's right hand, grabbed his left arm and pointed the empty pistol at the madman.

'Simon Carew you are under arrest! Anything you say …'

Hetherington read him his rights. Fortunately, Carew was only a small guy and with a pistol at his head, although continuing to struggle, he realised the game was up. He just stared and gave a maniacal grin. Still holding the pistol, Donald shouted through the open window. 'I've got him! Can somebody bring the cuffs, quickly!'

*　　*　　*

Nobody noticed the dirty, very off-yellow Ford Escort that had discreetly followed the Police convoy until the last mile. With the aid of an OS map, Hobson had diverted off along a gravel track that swung round to the back of the Newman's farm and parked on a small incline from where he could look down on the whole scene. He had left the car and moved forward until he had a view, with binoculars, of the window where Carew fondled his gun.

'Oh my God!' Hobson could see what was beginning to develop. He then saw Hetherington crawling through the undergrowth. He wondered if they realised how prepared Carew was and if he should attempt to warn the coppers of what he could see. Yet the journalist in him took over. Here was a scoop and he was there to capture it. If any of the Police were shot, then he would snap it to make the story even more sensational and earn himself an even fatter pay-off from hawking it around the tabloids to the highest bidder. Hobson took out his SLR zoom camera and waited.

*   *   *

'Well, they've got him …'

Kelvin looked at the front pages of the several newspapers, especially the red tops. At her request, he had stayed with Charlotte and slept a rough night on the same sofa that Georgio had nearly destroyed. The poor girl was terrified, especially as there was the possibility of a second lunatic murderer posing a threat. On the front pages of most of the papers there was an enlarged, hazy picture of Simon Carew at the window holding his gun at the ready. On inside pages there were, variously, several photographs of Hetherington bringing him, handcuffed, out to Thomas and the waiting team. There were some cheesy headlines of 'Donald the Duck' type, indicating how Hetherington might well have been a sitting target. Yet, in all events, he was momentarily a national hero and his life would, arguably, not be the same for a long time.

'Wish you were photographed?' Charlotte asked.

'Nah, more important that I looked out for you, did my bit towards it.'

'I think you're all very brave.' Charlotte gave McQuaid a hug. 'And thanks a million: will you stay with me for a while longer?'

'Sure,' Kelvin beamed. 'Maybe I'll check out from the pub.'

*   *   *

Georgio sat in the police cell planning how he would get out of this goddamned mess. He was wealthy, Carl had seen to that, yet Rossini was both the solution and the problem and he would not be banged up in this god awful British nick if it had not been for Carl's obsessive stupidity. He had often wondered if his boss had been working for some higher authority and now the stupid bastard was dead. Georgio would contact the mob. He had money and they had power. After all, he had not actually done anything wrong or killed anybody, and he did not want to, anyway. Charlotte was a beautiful woman and if he had not been gay, he would have shagged her himself ... all he had done was to stand there with a fucking gun and then give himself up. Surely they couldn't hold him for that?

He shouted for the Sergeant who seemed to be in charge. 'Can you get me to a phone, or give me my mobile? I need to call America, need a lawyer, need ...'

He was really pissed off.

Chapter 26

In the shed, he looked down at his hands. The fingers of the left one were almost completely closed. The right hand would be kept free to execute the deed.

'It is nearly time,' he said. 'The fool, our pot-smoking brother Carew, has served Your purpose, as it was intended, to divert attention from what it is now necessary to do and his deeds have covered up mine. There are forces, especially in primitive societies, which partly emulate You throughout the world, yet which sometimes veer towards good and thus present a challenge. This was clearly the case when our other apostle, Rossini, was stopped in his tracks, enough to hesitate and then be shot. Through the Mafia, he was a major force in Your plans to finally control the world and must be avenged. There was powerful magic there and although it is difficult to eliminate the sources of such, the Witch Doctors, the Shamans, the Medicine Men, the Machis … I can eliminate this disciple who is the only one to practise in the civilised world, deriving his ancient power from the primitive one. He is more clever than he thinks and poses a huge threat to all that You are … he must now be urgently dealt with.'

* * *

Lionel sat in his chair and watched the lunchtime news. He felt so sad to see Simon Carew being dragged along cuffed to a burly woman police officer. 'They give less resistance,' Thomas was to tell him later, 'if cuffed to bit of skirt.'

Nevertheless, Lionel had always tried to encourage Simon and had felt sorry for him. With his stutter and obvious incompetence as a dancer, he afforded Hetherington the apparent delight of bullying him. How ironic it was that Donald should have been the one to arrest and bring him in, and now Lionel was finding it difficult to come to terms with the fact that this lost little boy could be capable of such horrendous murders. Even the power of the Machi had not warned him about Carew. The *kultrun* had, however, pointed to the evil of another and this was what was worrying him. Farnsworth had not been killed by Simon. 'Who the hell, then?' he asked himself. 'Who is the other murderer in our midst, and what is his purpose and motive?' Palfrey was a worried man.

* * *

Anthony Barrington was disturbed. Upon reading all the Police reports, forensic details and documents pertaining to the horrific Suffolk murders and the fact that there was, in all probability, another killer at large, the Home Secretary was far from happy. 'Not on my bloody watch!' he yelled at his Junior Ministers 'This fucking mess needs sorting, if the public are to have any confidence in this Government's ability to maintain law and order, especially in such an idyllic place as sleepy old Suffolk. And another thing,' Barrington added, 'I've had a call from the US Ambassador, we need to keep our Yankee friends happy, and they're upset about this Georgio bastard being kept in British Police custody. The top Washington defence lawyer, Babachek, is in mid-Atlantic right now, on his way to demand his release. Not sure who's financing him but the guy is a legal hot-shot who terrifies everybody, including, apparently, the White House itself, and takes no prisoners. If you pardon the pun! I've agreed with the Ambassador that the simplest solution is to let fucking

Georgio be extradited back to the States and let them deal with whatever crime they might agree that he's committed, but his involvement in the whole sorry business is a grey area and one that we would be well advised to get rid of. Thank you gentlemen, see to it!' He gave additional orders to the Private Secretaries.

Chapter 27

Thomas had given up. On the plus side, they had solved the horrific murders of the two Newmans as well as that of Andrew Carew, about which Williams was ecstatic. 'Bloody good way to end my career, before retiring,' he'd said.

Simon Carew, on Lionel Palfrey's legal advice, although stuttering, had pleaded guilty on the grounds of insanity and was incarcerated in Broadmoor. During his routine admission medical examination, the attending Doctor was mystified by some strange markings on various private parts of his body.

For a while the Police had basked in the success of being front-page news and interviewed on most television channels.

On the minus side, however, it greatly disturbed Thomas that Farnsworth's killer was still at large. Carew had vehemently denied his murder. 'Corin was my one friend,' he had protested. 'And someone copied my method, oh how I did enjoy burying those bastards alive, especially my brother,' he had told Thomas when being questioned.

'He was completely barking mad,' the Chief Super later told Detective Sergeant Hetherington, who he had promoted into his CID Team. Even a feature about Corin Farnsworth on *Crimewatch* had failed to attract a single phone call. Nobody had any clue as to who the mystery assailant with the spade and belladonna poison might have been on that dreadful windswept and rainy summer's night on the lonely forest road.

* * *

The whole series of horrific events had been devastating for the hitherto peaceful little backwater haven of Thorpe Amberley. Little did any of the village know that it was all part of a much bigger, terrifying set of forces which spanned the centuries, time and space, and which, for diverse reasons, had chosen their small community to be a microcosm of the greater struggle.

* * *

In time, the Tamberleys were back to the routine of dancing out at village inns on balmy summer evenings. This cheered everybody up enormously, although few would have guessed at the wider implications of what they were watching. McQuaid, under the tutelage of his good friend Hetherington, had proved to be a rapid learner of Morris Dancing and had progressed to becoming an extremely competent Fool. 'Least I can do, to carry on the work of Corin,' he had told Charlotte, with whom his close friendship was blossoming. Everything had fallen into place for him. Thomas had secured a job for him as a DC on his team and the American had taken over the rental of Farnsworth's cottage. He had applied for British citizenship and was enjoying being an honorary Englishman.

* * *

The troupe found themselves dancing outside The Cat one evening. 'Keep it in the village for a change,' Palfrey had commented. It was very hot and, as usual, nobody really wanted to dance inside the Stoat and they were all relieved when one of the normally quiet members of the side volunteered. As things got underway and both the Fool and

Stoat cavorted about to the delight of the crowd, nobody really took much notice of the fact that the Stoat moved away, closer to Palfrey, in one of the more complex tracking routines. The small man inside held up its frame with his right hand while his left hand clutched a hypodermic needle. The village crowd gasped and then applauded as the Stoat tripped and fell to the ground, obviously thinking that this was a new twist to the performance that they had all seen so many times before. Yet, for a while, the dancing continued and the Morris Men were unaware that, deep inside Chilean Patagonia, another dance was taking place, with hand-kerchiefs and other paraphernalia, to the incessant beating of a drum, somewhere in the background.

McQuaid thought otherwise. He rushed over to the Stoat. The man inside gasped a last breath as the needle protruded from his stomach. 'Sorry, Master,' Kelvin heard him whisper.

Any regular observer of things, in two villages a few hundred miles apart, would have noticed that the figurines on the sides of their respective churches seemed to have developed a tear.

In the high forests of Chile, a very old lady smiled and clutched a withered breast with one hand, as if she had been stabbed by a knife. With the other hand, she beat frantically upon the *kultrun* drum.

Some members of the crowd saw Lionel Palfrey put both hands on his ears as if to try and stop some deafening noise.

*   *   *

The British Airways jumbo jet wheeled around New York City in its holding circuit prior to being given landing permission from Air traffic Control at Kennedy Airport. As the warning light came on, Georgio tried to fasten his seat belt, made difficult by being cuffed to the FBI man. 'Give it here,' instructed the officer as he tried to help.

As the plane flew down along the course of the Hudson River, there was a deafening blast which ripped apart the central fuselage, causing the aircraft to plunge into the murky waters of the river and explode. Nobody survived.

* * *

In two English churchyards, the tears on the figurines turned to evil smiles again.

'And now it begins,' said another Morris man to himself. He had traced his ancestry back to a non-Christian nobleman in the fourteenth century.

* * *

The friendship between the two Americans developed into a relationship in which they became an item. Some six months later, after a passionate night in bed, Charlotte gave a gasp as she watched breakfast television. The smell of bacon wafted from the kitchen as McQuaid was trying out his basic culinary skills.

'Kelvin!' she cried out. 'Come and look at this!'

A strange news story was breaking about mysterious deaths amongst those involved in paganism and quoted unconfirmed examples from Morris sides, druids and others in different parts of Britain.

Because of the dramatic events in their lives, they had also grown close to the otherwise quite lonely Mr Palfrey.

'Jesus!' Kelvin shouted. 'Better give Lionel a call, right now!'

The bacon was burnt.